JANE URQUHART

Jane Urquhart was born in Geraldton, Ontario, and grew up in Toronto. She has had published a collection of short stories, STORM GLASS, and three books of poetry, I AM WALKING IN THE GARDEN OF HIS IMAGINARY PALACE, FALSE SHUFFLES and THE LITTLE FLOWERS OF MADAME DE MONTESPAN. Her highly acclaimed second novel, CHANGING HEAVEN, was published in 1990 by Hodder and Stoughton and by Sceptre in paperback. She lives with her husband, artist Tony Urquhart, and their daughter Emily, in the village of Wellesley, Ontario.

sceptre

Jane Urquhart

THE WHIRLPOOL

Printed and bound in Great Britain for Hodder and Stoughton Paperbacks, a division of Hodder and Stoughton Ltd., Mill Road, Dunton Green, Sevenoaks, Kent TN13 2YA. (Editorial Office: 47 Bedford Square, London WC1B 3DP) by Clays Ltd., St Ives plc.

British Library C.I.P.

Urquhart, Jane
  The whirlpool.
  I. Title
  813'.54[F]

ISBN 0-340-53087-1

This book is for Stuart MacKinnon with thanks

ACKNOWLEDGMENTS

I would like to thank the many friends who encouraged and advised me as I worked my way through the several drafts of this book; Janet Turnbull for fishing it out of a whirlpool filled with many other manuscripts, Geoff Hancock for his continued support over the last several years, Stuart MacKinnon, Virgil Burnett, Rikki Ducornet, and Michael Ondaatje for their careful readings, and finally Ellen Seligman at McClelland and Stewart without whose tireless efforts this novel might never have been finished at all.

Also, deep gratitude goes to the Canada Council and the Ontario Arts Council for their financial support.

Short sections of this novel have appeared in slightly different form in *Descant*; *Canadian Fiction Magazine*; *Poetry Canada Review*; and *Views from the North: An Anthology of Travel Writing* (Porcupine's Quill).

✤Prologue✤

In December of 1889, as he was returning by gondola from the general vicinity of the Palazzo Manzoni, it occurred to Robert Browning that he was more than likely going to die soon. This revelation had nothing to do with either his advanced years or the state of his health. He was seventy-seven, a reasonably advanced age, but his physical condition was described by most of his acquaintances as vigorous and robust. He took a cold bath each morning and every afternoon insisted on a three-mile walk during which he performed small errands from a list his sister had made earlier in the day. He drank moderately and ate well. His mind was as quick and alert as ever.

Nevertheless, he knew he was going to die. He also had to admit that the idea had been with him for some time – two or three months at least. He was not a man to ignore symbols, especially when they carried personal messages. Now he had to acknowledge that the symbols were in the air as surely as winter. Perhaps, he speculated, a man carried the seeds of his death with him always, somewhere buried in his brain, like the face of a woman he is going to love. He leaned to one side, looked into the deep waters of the canal, and saw his own face reflected there. As broad and distinguished and cheerful as ever, health shining vigorously, robustly from his eyes, even in such a dark mirror.

Empty Gothic and Renaissance palaces floated on either side of him like soiled pink dreams. Like sunsets with dirty faces, he mused, and then, pleased with the phrase, he reached into his jacket for his notebook, ink pot, and pen. He had trouble recording the words, however, as the chill in the air had numbed his hands. Even the ink seemed affected by the cold, not flowing as smoothly as usual. He wrote slowly and deliberately, making sure to add the exact time and the location. Then he closed the book and returned it with the pen and pot to his pocket, where he curled and uncurled his right hand for some minutes until he felt the circulation return to normal. The celebrated Venetian dampness was much worse in winter, and Browning began to look forward to the fire at his son's palazzo where they would be beginning to serve afternoon tea, perhaps, for his benefit, laced with rum.

A sudden wind scalloped the surface of the canal. Browning instinctively looked upwards. Some blue patches edged by ragged white clouds, behind them wisps of grey and then the solid dark strip of a storm front moving slowly up on the horizon. Such a disordered sky in this season. No solid, predictable blocks of weather with definite beginnings, definite endings. Every change in the atmosphere seemed an emotional response to something that had gone before. The light, too, harsh and metallic, not at all like the golden Venice of summer. There was something broken about all of it, torn. The sky, for instance, was like a damaged canvas. Pleased again by his own metaphorical thoughts, Browning considered reaching for the notebook. But the cold forced him to reject the idea before it had fully formed in his mind.

Instead, his thoughts moved lazily back to the place they had been when the notion of death so rudely interrupted them; back to the building he had just visited. Palazzo Manzoni. *Bella, bella* Palazzo Manzoni! The colourful marble medallions rolled across Browning's inner eye, detached from their home on the Renaissance façade, and he began, at once, to reconstruct for the thousandth time the imaginary windows and balconies he had planned for the building's restoration. In his daydreams the old poet had walked over the palace's swollen marble floors and slept beneath its frescoed ceilings, lit fires underneath its sculptured mantels and entertained guests by the light of its chandeliers. Surrounded by a small crowd of admirers he had read poetry aloud in the evenings, his voice echoing through the halls. *No R.B. tonight*, he had said to them, winking. *Let's have some real poetry*. Then, moving modestly into the palace's impressive library, he had selected a volume of Dante or Donne.

But they had all discouraged him and it had never come to pass. Some of them said that the façade was seriously cracked and the foundations were far from sound. Others told him that the absentee owner would never part with it for anything resembling a fair price. Eventually, friends and family wore him down with their disapproval and, on their advice, he abandoned his daydream though he still made an effort to visit it, despite the fact that it was now damaged and empty and the glass in its windows was broken.

It was the same kind of frustration and melancholy that he associated with his night dreams of Asolo, the little hill town he had first seen (and only then at a distance), when he was twenty-six years old. Since that time, and for no rational reason, it had appeared over and over in the poet's dreams as a destination on the horizon, one that, due to a variety of circumstances, he was never able to reach. Either his companions in the dream would persuade him to take an alternate route, or the road would be impassable, or he would awaken just as the town gate came into view, frustrated and out of sorts. "I've had my old Asolo dream again," he would tell his sister at breakfast, "and it has no doubt ruined my work for the whole day."

Then, just last summer, he had spent several months there at the home of a friend. The house was charming and the view of the valley delighted him. But, although he never once broke the well-established order that ruled the days of his life, a sense of unreality clouded his perceptions. He was visiting the memory of a dream with a major and important difference. He had reached the previously elusive hill town with practically no effort. Everything had proceeded according to plan. Thinking about this, under the December sky in Venice, Browning realized that he had known since then that it was only going to be a matter of time.

The gondola bumped against the steps of his son's palazzo.

Robert Browning climbed onto the terrace, paid the gondolier, and walked briskly inside.

Lying on the magnificent carved bed in his room, trying unsuccessfully to partake of his regular pre-dinner nap, Robert Browning examined his knowledge like a stolen jewel he had coveted for years; turning it first this way, then that, imagining the reactions of his friends, what his future biographers would have to say about it all. He was pleased that he had prudently written his death poem at Asolo in direct response to having received a copy of Tennyson's "Crossing the Bar" in the mail. How he detested that poem! What *could* Alfred have been thinking of when he wrote it? He had to admit, nonetheless, that to suggest that mourners restrain their sorrow, as Tennyson had, guarantees the floodgates of female tears will eventually burst open. His poem had, therefore, included similar sentiments, but without, he hoped, such obvious sentimentality. It was the final poem of his last manuscript which was now, mercifully, at the printer's.

Something for the biographers and for the weeping maidens; those who had wept so copiously for his dear-departed, though soon to be reinstated wife. Surely it was not too much to ask that they might shed a few tears for him as well, even if his was a more ordinary death, following, he winced to have to add, a fairly conventional life.

How had it all happened? He had placed himself in the centre of some of the world's most exotic scenery and had then lived his life there with the regularity of a copy clerk. A time for everything, everything in its time. Even when hunting for lizards in Asolo, an occupation he considered slightly exotic, their appearance seemed somehow predictable; as if they knew he was searching for them and assembled their modest population at the sound of his footsteps. Even so, he was able to flush out only six or seven from a hedge of considerable length and these were, more often than not, of the same type. Once he thought he had seen a particularly strange lizard, large and lumpy, but it had turned out to be merely two of the ordinary sort, copulating.

Copulation. What sad dirge-like associations the word dredged up in the poet's unconscious. All those Italians; those minstrels, dukes, princes, artists, and questionable monks whose voices had droned through Browning's pen over the years. Why had they all been so endlessly obsessed with the subject? He could never understand or control it. And even now, one of them had appeared in full period costume in his imagination. A duke, no doubt, by the look of the yards of velvet which covered his person. He was reading a letter that was causing him a great deal of pain. Was it a letter from his mistress? A draught of poison waited on an intricately tooled small table to his left. Perhaps a pistol or a dagger as well, but in this light Browning could not quite tell. The man paced, paused, looked wistfully out the window as if waiting for someone he knew would never, ever appear. Very, very soon now he would begin to speak, to tell his story. His right hand passed nervously across his eyes. He turned to look directly at Robert Browning who, as always, was beginning to feel somewhat embarrassed. Then the duke began:

At last to leave these darkening moments
These rooms, these halls where once
We stirred love's poisoned potions
The deepest of all slumbers,
After this astounds the mummers
I cannot express the smile that circled
Round and round the week
This room and all our days when morning
Entered, soft, across her cheek.
She was my medallion, my caged dove,
A trinket, a coin I carried warm,
Against the skin inside my glove
My favourite artwork was a kind of jail
Our portrait permanent, imprinted by the moon
Upon the ancient face of the canal.

The man began to fade. Browning, who had not invited him into the room in the first place, was already bored. He therefore dismissed the crimson costume, the table, the potion housed in its delicate goblet of fine Venetian glass and began, quite inexplicably, to think about Percy Bysshe Shelley; about his life, and under the circumstances, more importantly, about his death.

Dinner over, sister, son and daughter-in-law and friend all chatted with and later read to, Browning returned to his room with Shelley's death hovering around him like an annoying, directionless wind. He doubted as he put on his nightgown, that Shelley had *ever* worn one, particularly in those dramatic days preceding his early demise. In his night cap he felt as ridiculous as a humorous political drawing for *Punch* magazine. And, as he lumbered into bed alone, he remembered that Shelley would have had Mary beside him and possibly Clare as well, their minds buzzing with nameless Gothic terrors. For a desperate moment or two

Browning tried to conjure a Gothic terror but discovered, to his great disappointment, that the vague shape taking form in his mind was only his dreary Italian duke coming, predictably, once again into focus.

Outside the ever calm waters of the canal licked the edge of the terrace in a rhythmic, sleep-inducing manner; a restful sound guaranteeing peace of mind. But Browning knew, however, that during Shelley's last days at Lerici, giant waves had crashed into the ground floor of Casa Magni, prefiguring the young poet's violent death and causing his sleep to be riddled with wonderful nightmares. Therefore, the very lack of activity on the part of the water below irritated the old man. He began to pad around the room in his bare feet, oblivious to the cold marble floor and the dying embers in the fireplace. He peered through the windows into the night, hoping that he, like Shelley, might at least see his double there, or possibly Elizabeth's ghost beckoning to him from the centre of the canal. He cursed softly as the night gazed back at him, serene and cold and entirely lacking in events – mysterious or otherwise.

He returned to the bed and knelt by its edge in order to say his evening prayers. But he was completely unable to concentrate. Shelley's last days were trapped in his brain like fish in a tank. He saw him surrounded by the sublime scenery of the Ligurian coast, searching the horizon for the boat which was to be his coffin. Then he saw him clinging desperately to the mast of that boat while lightning tore the sky in half and the ocean spilled across the hull. Finally, he saw Shelley's horrifying corpse rolling on the shoreline, practically unidentifiable except for the copy of Keats' poems housed in his breast pocket. *Next to his heart*, Byron had commented, just before he got to work on the funeral pyre.

Browning abandoned God for the moment and climbed beneath the blankets.

"I might at least have a nightmare," he said petulantly to himself. Then he fell into a deep and dreamless sleep.

Browning awakened the next morning with an itchy feeling in his throat and lines from Shelley's *Prometheus Unbound* dancing in his head.

"Oh God," he groaned inwardly, "now this. And I don't even *like* Shelley's poetry anymore. Now I suppose I'm going to be plagued with it, day in, day out, until the instant of my imminent death."

How he wished he had never, ever, been fond of Shelley's poems. Then, in his youth, he might have had the common sense *not* to read them compulsively to the point of total recall. But how could he have known in those early days that even though he would later come to reject both Shelley's life and work as being "too impossibly self-absorbed and emotional," some far corner of his brain would still retain every syllable the young man put to paper. He had memorized his life's work. Shortly after Browning's memory recited *The crawling glaciers pierce me with spears / Of their moon freezing crystals, the bright chains / Eat with their burning cold into my bones*, he began to cough, a spasm that lasted until his sister knocked discreetly on the door to announce that, since he had not appeared downstairs, his breakfast was waiting on a tray in the hall.

While he was drinking his tea, the poem "Ozymandius" repeated itself four times in his mind except that, to his great annoyance, he found that he could not remember the last three lines and kept ending with *Look on my works, ye Mighty, and despair*. He knew for certain that there were three more lines, but he was damned if he could recall even one of them. He thought of asking his sister but soon realized that, since she was familiar with his views on Shelley, he would be forced to answer a series of embarrassing questions about why he was thinking about the poem at all. Finally, he decided that *Look on my works, ye Mighty, and despair* was a much more fitting ending to the poem and attributed his lack of recall to the supposition that the last three lines were either unsuitable or completely unimportant. That settled, he wolfed down his roll, donned his hat and coat, and departed for the streets in hopes that something, anything, might happen.

Even years later, Browning's sister and son could still be counted upon to spend a full evening discussing what he might have done that day. The possibilities were endless. He might have gone off hunting for a suitable setting for a new poem, or for the physical characteristics of a duke by examining handsome northern Italian workmen. He might have gone, again, to visit his beloved Palazzo Manzoni, to gaze wistfully at its marble medallions. He might have gone to visit a Venetian builder, to discuss plans for the beautiful tower he had talked about building at Asolo, or out to Murano to watch men mould their delicate bubbles of glass. His sister was convinced that he had gone to the Church of S.S. Giovanni e Paolo to gaze at his favourite equestrian statue. His pious son, on the other hand, liked to believe that his father had spent the day in one of the few English churches in Venice, praying for the redemption of his soul. But all of their speculations assumed a sense of purpose on the poet's part, that he had left the house with a definite destination in mind, because as long as they could remember, he had never acted without a predetermined plan.

Without a plan, Robert Browning faced the Grand Canal with very little knowledge of what, in fact, he was going to do. He looked to the left, and then to the right, and then, waving aside an expectant gondolier, he turned abruptly and entered the thick of the city behind him. There he wandered aimlessly through a labyrinth of narrow streets, noting details; putti wafting stone garlands over windows, door knockers in the shape of gargoyles' heads, painted windows which fooled the eye, items which two weeks earlier would have delighted him but which now seemed used and lifeless. Statues appeared to leak and ooze damp soot, window-glass was fogged with moisture, steps which led him over canals slippery, covered with an unhealthy slime. He became peculiarly aware of the smells which he had previously ignored in favour of the more pleasant sensations the city had to offer. But now even the small roof gardens seemed to grow as if in stagnant water, winter chrysanthemums emitting a putrid odour which spoke less of blossom than decay. With a kind of slow horror, Browning realized that he was seeing his beloved city through Shelley's eyes and immediately his inner voice began again: *Sepulchres where human forms / Like pollution nourished worms / To the corpse of greatness cling / Murdered and now mouldering.*

He quickened his steps, hoping that if he concentrated on physical activity his mind would not subject him to the complete version of Shelley's "Lines Written Among the Euganean Hills." But he was not to be spared. The poem had been one of his favourites in his youth and, as a result, his mind was now capable of reciting it to him, word by word, with appropriate emotional inflections, followed by a particularly moving rendition of "Julian and Maddalo" accompanied by mental pictures of Shelley and Byron galloping along the beach at the Lido.

When at last the recitation ceased, Browning had walked as far as possible and now found himself at the edge of the Fondamente Nuove with only the wide, flat expanse of the Laguna Morta in front of him.

He surveyed his surroundings and began, almost unconsciously, and certainly against his will, to search for the islanded madhouse that Shelley had described in "Julian and Madallo": *A building on an island; such a one / As age to age might add, for uses vile / A windowless, deformed and dreary pile.* Then he remembered, again against his will, that it was on the other side, near the Lido. Instead, his eyes came to rest on the cemetery island of San Michele whose neat, white mausoleums and tidy cypresses looked fresher, less sepulchral than any portion of the city he had passed through. Although he had never been there he could tell, even from this distance, that its paths would be raked and its marble scrubbed in a way that the rest of Venice never was. Like a disease that cannot cross the water, the rot and mould of the city had never reached the cemetery's shore.

It pleased Browning, now, to think of the island's clean-boned inhabitants sleeping in their white-washed houses. Then, his mood abruptly changing, he thought with disgust of Shelley, of his bloated corpse upon the sands, how the experience of his flesh had been saturated by water, then burned away by fire, and how his heart had refused to burn as if it had not been made of flesh at all.

Browning felt the congestion in his chest take hold, making his breathing shallow and laboured, and he turned back into the city, attempting to determine the direction of his son's palazzo. Pausing now and then to catch his breath, he made his way slowly through the streets that make up the Fondamente Nuove, an area with which he was completely unfamiliar. This was Venice at its most squalid. What little elegance had originally existed in this section had now faded so dramatically that it had all but disappeared. Scrawny children screamed and giggled on every narrow walkway and tattered washing hung from most windows. In doorways, sullen elderly widows stared insolently and with increasing hostility at this obvious foreigner who had invaded their territory. A dull panic began to overcome him as he realized he was lost. The disease meanwhile had weakened his legs, and he stumbled awkwardly under the communal gaze of these women who were like black angels marking his path. Eager to be rid of their judgmental stares, he turned into an alley, smaller than the last, and found to his relief that it was deserted and graced with a small fountain and a stone bench.

The alley, of course, was blind, went nowhere, but it was peaceful and Browning was in need of rest. He leaned back against the stone wall and closed his eyes. The fountain murmured *Bysshe, Bysshe, Bysshe* until the sound finally became soothing to Browning and he dozed, on and off, while fragments of Shelley's poetry moved in and out of his consciousness.

Then, waking suddenly from one of these moments of semi-slumber, he began to feel again that he was being watched. He searched the upper windows and the doorways around him for old women and found none. Instinctively, he looked at an archway which was just a fraction to the left of his line of vision. There, staring directly into his own, was the face of Percy Bysshe Shelley, as young and sad and powerful as Browning had ever known it would be. The visage gained flesh and expression for a glorious thirty seconds before returning to the marble that it really was. With a sickening and familiar sense of loss, Browning recognized the carving of Dionysus, or Pan, or Adonis that often graced the tops of Venetian doorways. The sick old man walked toward it and, reaching up, placed his fingers on the soiled cheek. "Suntreader," he mumbled, then he moved out of the alley, past the black, disapproving women, into the streets towards a sizeable canal. There, bent over his walking stick, coughing spasmodically, he was able to hail a gondola.

All the way back across the city he murmured, "Where have you been, where have you been, where did you go?"

⌀

*"For everyone
The swimmer's moment at the whirlpool comes"*

– Margaret Avison

At Halstead in England, during the last half of the nineteenth century, employees at Courtauld Limited wove secret cloth on secret looms in secret factories. Warp, woof . . . warp, woof. Like makers of Venetian glass they were devoted to their craft and frightened of their masters. They took, therefore, the coveted recipe for crape with them to their graves. The Courtaulds held the monopoly in mourning garb; it was the key to their immense fortune, and they wanted to make absolutely sure that they kept it.

The workers – mute, humble, and underpaid – spent twelve hours a day, in hideous conditions, at their steam-powered looms pounding black silk threads into acres of unpleasant cloth. In ten years, enough crape had been produced to completely cover the province of Quebec. In twenty, the whole empire could have been wrapped; a depressing parcel with a black sheen.

Still, death being what it is, there was often not enough cloth to go around. After major epidemics, or during wars, women would be forced to have their mourning attire made of less prestigious fabrics; bombazine or, in desperation, black cotton or wool. Men never had this problem. The same black hat-band did well for each bereavement.

Real crape did not hang down in smooth, graceful folds like cotton. It did not cuddle like wool. It encased the female body, instead, in a suit of crumpled armour, tarnished to a dull black. It scraped at the neck and dug at the armpits. It clung to the limbs and rasped at the shoulder blades. It lacerated the spine if that series of bones ever dared to relax. And it smelled, always, of grave mud and sorrow.

In Niagara Falls, Canada, the undertaker's widow, Maud Grady, was forced to wrap herself in real Courtauld crape. No cheap, comfortable imitations for her; she felt duty bound to set an example. The perfect symbol of animate deep mourning, she wore crimped crape for two full years, adding, when the first few months had passed, some jet beads and a small amount of fringe to her costume. Much of her average day was spent organizing the paraphernalia of bereavement: black parasol, black stockings, underwear edged in black ribbon, black-framed stationery, black ink making black words, black sealing wax, black veil, black bonnet tied under the chin in a menacing black bow. The child, too, she dressed in crape for the first six months, moving to greys and mauves when that period was over.

It hadn't been at all pleasant. Apart from the physical discomfort, there was the accompanying fear of weather; of heat and of precipitation. The smallest bit of moisture, fog, or even minor amounts of perspiration would cause the colour of the fabric to bleed through to her skin until, some nights when she undressed, her body looked as if it had been the victim of a severe beating. For a while she made use of a smelly concoction of tartar and oxalic acid in an attempt to remove the stains. Finally, however, despite a liberal sprinkling of rosewater, her whole bedroom reeked of chemicals. At that point she decided to let the black marks on her skin accumulate. Who would know? Who would care? She could fix it all later, if she survived.

At night, she dreamed dreams about her dead husband. Often he appeared in the very bedroom where she slept to announce that he had just died and would be busy for the next few days embalming himself and arranging his own funeral. He always had a black band wound around his hat out of respect for his own passing and a look on his face of profound sorrow. Maud would offer him a cape made of crape but he would reject it, outright, as if it had been something intended for the opera. Guiltily, in the dream, after this refusal, Maud would once again drape the heavy material on her own shoulders realizing, as she did so, where it rightfully belonged.

He walked through her dreams in a shroud of thick webs. There was nothing ghoulish about this, nothing even surprising. Apart from the art of embalming, his only interest had been in the habits of spiders. During his short adulthood he had studied them obsessively, collecting members of the species, recording their activities in a growing series of notebooks.

After two or three months of widowhood and strange dreams, Maud decided to have an elaborate brooch made out of a lock of her husband's hair, his dead hair; an oval frame of gold would surround two desolate hairy willows which would, in turn, flank a hairy tombstone with his initials on it. All of this was to be placed under a bubble of thin glass; a sort of transparent barrier between that tiny hairy world of graves and weeping and the one that Maud walked around in every day. A barrier, but one that was easy enough to see through nonetheless.

Once the piece of jewellery was fabricated, she pinned it, after nightmares, at her gradually blackening throat each morning. Looking at herself and at the oval jewel in the centre of her collar in the mirror, she had to admit that one of the hairy willows looked remarkably like a spider that had been captured, chloroformed, and kept.

He had died on the same day as his parents. The epidemic, carried by him into the house after contact with a corpse, had spread like a fog into the three related sets of lungs, leaving Maud and the child (then two) completely untouched – not even a sniffle.

Maud, shock having cancelled fear, had nursed them all ... had watched them die. She would always remember how the child stared from three separate doorways, his eyes widening when the convulsions set in. It simply had not occurred to her to remove him from the scene. Besides, there was no one to tend to him. The staff had decided to remain at home rather than risk the disease.

Oddly, she would also always remember the colours each of the dying faces had turned during the throes: Charles' green; her mother-in-law's red; and her father-in-law's purple. Emotional, really, she had thought at the time, and quite in keeping with their personalities: Charles resigned; her mother-in-law flustered; her father-in-law furious with anything he couldn't control. While one half of Maud's brain turned to ice at the horror, the other remained curious and alert. Details, such as the way that hands picked at bedclothes or the way heads dented pillows, absorbed her. She found herself counting the number of seconds which passed between one dying breath and the next. Until there was no breath left at all.

All over town, behind shades drawn against the sun, people were dying. Maud knew the significance of the repetitive knocking at her door, knew parents and children were seeking the services of the undertaking establishment. She did not, could not, answer with three of her own dying upstairs and her heart inhabiting some other land where explanations were impossible. She found herself thinking of burial practices during medieval plagues; carts filled with bodies destined for huge, hastily dug pits. *Bring out your dead. Bring out your dead.*

Charles died first. He inhaled deeply and smoothly, his first unlaboured breath for hours, opened his eyes, looked directly at Maud with an even gaze and, just as one heartbeat of hope reached her breast, he shrugged and disappeared, leaving behind a body that she hardly recognized.

His parents were more conventional. They gurgled and rattled appropriately before collapsing into absence. Maud left each of them alone, untouched, in their separate rooms with their eyes open.

Outside, the glorious weather of late spring continued as if nothing at all had changed – shadows of low, white, fluffy clouds on the garden and all the fruit trees in full bloom. For the first twelve hours after those dramatic morning deaths Maud spent her time at windows, the child near her skirts, silent, almost forgotten. She watched the yard all afternoon, noting how the sun moved, lending light to first one, then another of the flower-beds. The wind changed at some point and all the plants that had previously bent to the west began to bend to the east. Birds arrived and departed. A rabbit ate a third of the first crop of lettuce in the vegetable garden, unhurriedly, as if he knew he would not be disturbed.

In the early evening she walked into the sunroom at the opposite side of the house and looked down at the street, very empty now because of the epidemic. The breeze had picked up considerably and little whirlwinds of dust, mixed with a few petals from apple blossoms, moved quietly down Main Street. Most of the shops were closed and the rocking chairs on the verandah of Kick's Hotel were all vacant. For a moment or two Maud wondered if she and the child were the sole survivors, if bedrooms all over town were filled with corpses. Then a streetcar rumbled into sight, occupied by three or four apparently healthy passengers.

She was still gazing through glass when the gas-lamps were lit. These sudden illuminations caused her to stir and stretch and begin to move around the house. Wandering from room to room of the building that had never belonged to her, lighting lamp after lamp, Maud stared at the possessions of her in-laws which, in their haphazard placement, had become a kind of testimonial to the rapidity of the disease. The account book open on the desk in the sunroom where Charles had left it, her father-in-law's pipe resting in a bowl in the parlour, her mother-in-law's unfinished embroidery, the needle halted in mid-stitch. She decided to visit, for the first time, the storage room at the back of the building where the strange, relatively new embalming equipment was kept. Just three years ago, Charles and his friend Sam had received an embalming certificate, each, from the school in Rochester. In order to avoid the inevitable loss of income that would be the result of Charles' friend opening up his own business, the elder Mr. Grady had immediately hired him. Now Sam would be the only licenced embalmer in Canada.

In the small manufactory adjacent to the storage room, Maud examined coffins. She ran her hands along the smooth wood and downy velvet she had never dared to touch, wondering if Jas the carpenter had survived the sickness and, if so, what kind of boxes he would choose, or prepare, for her husband and in-laws upstairs. Humorous stories she had heard Charles repeat ran inexplicably through her mind: coffins too short or too narrow for certain individuals; dignified military officers with maggots crawling out of their ears; the time that Charles' father had backed accidentally into a grave, smashing the coffin and causing even the most grief-stricken mourners to titter.

During that first long night, while the child slept, Maud brought every moveable source of light into the parlour and there, surrounded by scores of candles and several coal-oil lamps, she began to play the piano – loudly, fiercely. By four in the morning she had exhausted her entire repertoire; all of the Canadian Hymnal and the few pieces of classical music she had learned as a girl. At regular intervals she played and sang "God Save the Queen." Once she rose from the piano bench to close the doors of the three rooms where her family lay. She didn't, somehow, want to disturb them.

At six a.m., after playing the hymn "Unto the Hills" for the ninth time, Maud abruptly left the piano, washed her face, ran a comb hastily through her hair, and descended the staircase that led to the world. Soon she was at Sam the embalmer's door, offering him a substantial raise in pay and a position as manager of the business. From there she went to the housekeeper's, to Jas the carpenter, and to the home of the man her father-in-law had hired to help in the garden and in the stables. Her conversations with these individuals were terse, perfunctory. Everyone was dead, she said, except for her and the child. She intended to survive, and it was her wish that the business should continue as usual. If they did not want to retain their positions they should tell her now so that she could replace them. If, however, they wished to stay on they should report for work in exactly one hour.

The house looked entirely different to her when she returned, as if the colours of the upholstered furniture had deepened, as if the patterns in the wallpaper had become more pronounced during her short absence. When she entered the child's room, vivid colour lithographs of harmless lambs and ponies seemed to leap at her from the walls in a menacing fashion. The child's own little face among the bedclothes was so startlingly beautiful, so vehemently alive, even in sleep, that, for a minute or so, Maud was afraid to waken him. By seven-thirty, however, she had him dressed and in the kitchen. There she quickly located the utensils which, until that moment, had been touched only by the house-keeper. While the child attacked a plateful of toast and jam and swallowed mugfuls of milk, Maud fixed herself a cup of strong coffee.

Half an hour later she was walking down the long, dark hall, past the three separate doors, into the brightness of the sunroom. She situated herself at Charles' desk in front of the open ledger. She flipped up the silver lid of his inkwell and lifted his pen in her hand.

When at the end of the morning she heard the men climb the stairs with their canvas stretchers, she leaned back exhausted in her husband's chair and surveyed her labours. She was amazed to see that she had brought the account book almost entirely up to date.

Today, exactly two years after the fatal date, was her first of half-mourning. Maud was able, therefore, to dress herself in a black and white cotton stripe, with long sleeves and a high neck, not neglecting, of course, the special brooch. She sat now in the sunroom, surrounded by the pungent aroma of the tartar and oxalic acid, which she had been scrubbing into her skin for most of the morning. The results had not been entirely satisfactory but she had succeeded, at last, in turning her upper torso from mottled black to spotty grey. Short of removing two layers of skin, she knew she would have to stop there for the time being.

She leaned back in the chair and felt the uncorseted part of her back respond to the cool cotton. Her greatest joy would come in the afternoon when, veilless, she would venture into the streets to do a few errands. For the past two years she had looked at the world beyond her walls through the permanent cloud of her black veil, occasionally latticed, when the wind blew them to the front, by the black ribbons, or weepers, from her oppressive bonnet. Not that she had gone far. Crape was not made for strolling about in. It clung to her black-stockinged thighs (her petticoat was made of the same fabric), while the weepers stuck to the material around her shoulders, making it impossible for her to move her head. This, combined with the partial blindness caused by the veil, had led her, more than once, into the path of an oncoming streetcar or carriage. Had it not been for her acute sense of hearing she might have joined her husband in Drummond Hill Cemetery months ago.

Just as she had done for the past two years, she was spending the morning working on accounts. But now she held the pen as easily as a teaspoon in her hand, and the scratch, scratch of the nib was as familiar as the sound of her own breathing. The dreams had subsided; Charles visiting her bedroom, now, only once or twice a month. It was as though he was forgetting her, she thought, rather irrationally, for, in truth, she was forgetting him. Not their time together but his physical actuality. She could no longer bring his face clearly into her mind. As time went by, in fact, Maud found it more and more difficult to believe that she had ever been married at all, more and more difficult to believe that the pen she held in her hand had not always been her own.

Disaster had not disappeared, but it had diminished in size, had become, in a sense, manageable; no larger than the words one might use to describe it.

Once she had settled herself in the streetcar, Fleda knew it would only be fifteen minutes or so until she was there. In her basket she had the makings of high tea; muffins, blueberry jam, sweet fresh butter, some mild cheese and the tea itself – a good Ceylonese blend. Under her arm, near her heart, she cradled a copy of Swinburne's *Poems and Ballads*, *The Ring and the Book* by Robert Browning, and Patmore's *Angel in the House*. She had brought the books along in order to read them in a suitable setting; a setting that she hoped was about to cause the spiritual marriage of romance and domesticity in her life.

The wheels of the trolley clattered under the boards at her feet. The vehicle had been scrubbed and polished, as if to celebrate the advent of the blossom season, and light bounced from brass fittings, glowed in the warmth of the wood at the top of the seats, and shone through the windows from which the glass had been removed. It was possible, in this slow-moving car, to lean out from open rectangles in order to pick blossoms from the trees that bordered the route. But Fleda's mind was in another location and she hardly noticed the lilacs, the cherry blossoms. An offensive man at the front of the car had twisted his thick torso at the waist so that he might eye her unashamedly while he breathed lungfuls of cigar smoke into the open air of the car. To her left, a very young couple was giggling over a photograph of themselves in front of a very bad reproduction of the waterfall. The beginning of the massive summer invasion. Fleda's thoughts turned to the whirlpool and an acre of land that rose from it. She was, at this moment, a woman on a streetcar with a whirlpool on her mind.

She was often, mentally, one or two steps ahead of her activities, her location. In the dark rooms that she had left behind in town she had anticipated the journey on the streetcar. Now, seated in the vehicle, she anticipated the arrival at her destination. After arrival, and a few brief moments of appreciation, anticipation would move swiftly into reflection. She kept a diary, and this, combined with her compulsive reading, had proved to be the perfect device for distancing synchronized response.

She checked her basket for this volume now, terrified for the moment that it might have been left behind. It was there, however, wedged between the muffins and the cheese. Relaxing, she turned at last to the window. The car had passed the city limits and was moving steadily down River Road into a rougher geography. If you avoided looking at the factories on the American side, you could almost believe you were in the wilderness. The tough old rocks of the escarpment were in evidence everywhere, varying in size from the jagged edges along the road to the cliffs that dropped down to the river. They poked, at times, through small patches of sumac or reared unexpectedly from clumps of long grass. The hill country of England, as Fleda imagined it, or gentle undulations of the Tuscan countryside, had nothing to do with this, nothing to do with this river side of the road. If she turned and looked through the windows on the opposite side of the car, however, she would see nothing but acres of rigidly planned, severely trimmed orchards. It was a geography of fierce opposites. Order on one side and, nearer the water, sublime geological chaos.

A cloud of cigar smoke passed between Fleda and the

scenery and escaped from the open window. She stood, pulled the wire for the bell, and walked towards the door, feeling, as she adjusted her body to the rocking of the car, the man's gaze at the back of her neck burning its way down her spine.

When the vehicle came to a halt Fleda stepped lightly to the ground and began, at once, to enter the woods in front of her. While she walked, she admired the carpet of trilliums that stretched out around her in all directions. The slow, quiet sound of the whirlpool began to reach her through the uniformly grey trunks of poplar and maple and ash which stood between her and the river. She dropped her belongings near the remains of an old dead fire, a relic of the previous summer's final event, and moved to the spot where the land began to tilt sharply downwards, a drop of three hundred feet. And even though the June foliage had thickened in earnest, she could see it clearly: the giant whirlpool – a cumbersome, magnificent merry-go-round on which a few large logs were seemingly permanent passengers. The awkward, ceaseless motion of going nowhere, the peace of it seen from above. Fleda stared down at the water for a good ten minutes then, shaking her head as if to throw off a trance, she returned to the place where she had left her basket. She placed her notebook and pencil on top of the three books she had brought with her and began, methodically, to gather twigs to make a fire for the tea.

Soon she had constructed a small, lopsided, teepee-like structure out of the delicate dead branches which were to be found everywhere on the ground around her. Then, after pausing for a moment, she rearranged them into a square formation, into what her husband called the log cabin method of building a fire. A tiny house, a doll's house; one that she would shortly have the pleasure of burning to the ground. She added some birch bark for a roof and, after a few frantic moments, when she believed she had forgotten her matches, she lit her miniature home. Her kettle hung from a pole suspended between two sticks which were planted in the ground and had survived the winter wonderfully well, buried, as they must have been, in the deep snow. She filled the kettle with rain water which had collected in a barrel situated several yards to her right, returned it to the pole overtop the flaming cabin, and began to search for the teapot. A few wooden crates were arranged neatly near the spot where she stood and under the third she uncovered four spoons, a small frying pan, and an earthenware pot. The other two boxes protected plates, cups, saucers, knives, forks, a spatula and a flower vase, all clean and ready for use, just as she had left them in September. Satisfied that her equipment was intact, she settled herself into a chair that had been hewn from a large stump, and waited for her kettle to boil.

While she waited she thought, with great pleasure, of the books she had brought with her; especially of the Browning, which she already knew well enough to look forward to. The Patmore, a small white volume with an embossed gold title, David had given to her that morning in their rooms, knowing she would want something to read while she waited for him, and feeling the subject suitable to the season when the house would be built. Fleda reached for this now and, flipping past the title page, turned to a reproduction of a portrait of the poet's wife by Rossetti. The Angel that had inhabited the House did not fare well under the harsh lines of the steel engraving, and Fleda secretly felt she looked more like a siren than an angel. She had constructed her own private, imaginary version of the woman's appearance and decided to hold to that now, despite this other, more ordinary evidence.

Fleda was deeply interested in this book, interested in the poet's perception of the perfect wife, his belief in matrimony as the heavenly ideal. Like a voyeur at the threshold of a fascinating window, her veins tingled with expectancy. By the time the tea was satisfactorily made, however, her mood had abruptly changed. A robin had settled briefly at her feet and then, surprised at what he found there, had quickly taken his leave. Intermittent clouds had begun to mask the sun and a breeze had turned the leaves of the poplars back, changing them from green to silver. Fleda walked a second time to the bank and looked down, through the network of branches, to the whirlpool. She could see a pillar of smoke ascending from the beach far below. Boys, who should be in school, fishing probably, cooking their catch. For a moment or two she thought of descending the bank, but remembered the previous weeks of rain, the mud on the path, and the fact that her yellow skirt and white boots were relatively new.

She returned to the fire, which was blazing nicely, and reached for her notebook and pencil. Turning to a fresh page she smoothed the spine of the book with her palm and wrote the date: 7 June 1889. She looked around her solemnly for a few moments, then she began to write.

In my twenty-seventh year and in good health I return to the Heights for the first time this year, and I begin again my summer diary.

D. has given me another book to read just this morning – Angel in the House by Patmore. A tribute to the poet's wife and her domestic demeanour. Just the ticket, D. says, since he thinks I am dangerously infatuated with the strange passions of Mr. Browning. Which, I suppose, I am.

By the end of the summer D. has promised (once again) that I shall have my own house here. The Patmore, I believe, was given to me as a sort of guarantee. I know, however, that he prefers the rooms in Kick's Hotel, since they are just across the street from the most cherished of his battlefields – Lundy's Lane. We'll see. I have already planned the views from each of the windows. The most wonderful collection of young birches, for instance, will lie just ten feet or so from the library windows. This will be large enough to let me read on winter days without the aid of artificial light. We will not, of course, be able to see the whirlpool anywhere, at any time from the house, but we shall always feel its influence, and, depending on the wind and the season, we shall be able at times to hear its cosmic music. D. does not believe that even when I am unable to hear the whirlpool because of wind and rain, I can still feel its music in the atmosphere. He claims that I have become deranged by reading too much of Mr. Browning and quotes some nonsense about angels beating their wings at the edge of the whirlpool in vain. I sincerely hope that D.'s ability as an historian is of a higher quality than his ability as a critic. It is Shelley's beating wings he is thinking of, not Browning's.

I note that Cedar Grove is unchanged, as dark and mysterious as ever. I regret now that I did not come to see it in the winter when the contrast of its branches against the white snow would have made a picture indeed. I feel sometimes that my own special group of cedars is trying desperately to become cosmopolitan, to resemble their Italian cousin, the cyprus, and it makes me glad since I believe it to be unlikely that I should ever be fortunate enough to travel to that enchanted land. Perhaps I should speak to the Scotch pines about umbrella pines in hopes they might take the suggestion. The Haunted Poplars, on the other hand, look strange with their new leaves just beginning. They seem much less haunted at this stage and do not produce, yet, the curious sound of a long dead court lady's skirts moving across a parquet floor.

I write this on my lap as I can see that the little desk which D. constructed for me at the edge of the bank on Lookout Point has toppled some time during the winter, probably under the weight of snow. But such a spot it is! If I lean to the left when I am sitting there I can see a good portion of the whirlpool through the trees, even when they are in full leaf. It is wonderful to sit there and read Browning . . . feeling as close to him as if he were a friend about to drop in for tea.

The winter was worse than usual. D. spent endless hours worrying about his research concerning the Siege of Fort Erie, so didn't mind the weather. I, on the other hand, unwilling to drink whiskey on the ice bridge with the tourists, spent my days trapped in that stuffy hotel, dreaming of the Heights and worrying about the birds here who were, no doubt, quite happy. Once or twice I took the streetcar to Queenston and realized, as I passed by, that this spot will be miraculously beautiful in winter . . . once I have my house.

"Shall I sonnet-sing you about myself?
Do I live in a house you would like to see?
Is it scant of gear, has it store or pelf?
Unlock my heart with a sonnet key."
R.B.   House

In any case, I can almost count myself an ex-prisoner of the hotel. D. has decided that this season we shall live here most of the time in a tent which he will borrow from the Camp at Niagara. It will be quite large since normally it houses ten soldiers and it will have a wooden floor. He intends to put it up this afternoon with the help of some of his men. Even if I do feel somewhat like a gypsy it will be better than suffering through another summer in town. It will not be habitable for a few days. D. intends to install a small stove with piping to help us through the chilly evenings. We will cook, of course, outside.

At this point, hearing horses, Fleda stopped writing. Her husband appeared at the end of the path that led to the road, mounted on a handsome stallion and looking proud and slightly pugnacious in his military attire. His face, however, carried an expression of warmth and tenderness, the object of which was his horse to whom he was speaking quietly. Behind him two of his men drove a wagon which carried a large canvas bundle and some lumber.

Fleda flung her notebook down to the ground and ran through the woods to greet them. She hadn't noticed that, while she was writing, her kettle had once again boiled, steamed ferociously, and cooled. The little house underneath it was now nothing more than a pile of ash.

◊

That's the way it was with Patrick. His response to stimuli was so finely tuned that even a change in geography might disorient him. The act of walking in the woods was made of a texture so different from the act of walking in the orchards that he knew some minutes would have to pass before he could relax enough to observe the birds he had come there to see, to collect wildflowers for his album.

He had walked out of the bright blaze of the orchard, across the road and the streetcar tracks, into the dark, cool forest. He was alone. His mind was adjusting to the change of light in the same way that the retinae of his eyes adjusted. Lenses opening in shadow.

Eventually he began to use the fieldglasses again as he had in the orchards, to follow the flights of birds. Moving the circular image across the trees in pursuit of a thrush, his vision brushed against a woman's face and it took several moments for him to accept what he had seen. He simply could not believe that she was real, could not, at first, cope with the fact of her being there. He refocused the instrument and moved it carefully back to the spot where her pale face had flickered. But by then she had disappeared. Finally, he spotted a portion of her blue dress, barely visible through the trees, and another piece of fabric of a tartan-like nature.

Patrick moved, quietly, a few feet closer. Crouching behind a sumac bush he, once again, brought the glasses up to his eyes. Now he could see her more clearly, her downcast face, the sunlight on her dark yellow hair. In this setting, surrounded by the yellow-green foliage of late spring and seated in blue shadows, she looked to him like a woman in a painting, as though she had been dropped into the middle of the scene for decorative purposes, or to play a part in a legend. Excited by these associations, he moved closer again. All the wildflower specimens he had collected fell, unnoticed, out of his pocket. A pink trillium was squashed under his right foot.

But now all he could see was the bottom of her blue skirt and her two leather boots, crossed at the ankles. Bending down he stepped, cautiously, several feet to the left and, safely disguised by a Scotch pine, he discovered with joy that the whole woman was within his range. She was sitting on a plaid blanket with her back against the trunk of a poplar, reading a leather-bound book. Her expression was one of great concentration.

Behind her stood a large white tent and directly in front of her a small campfire burned, causing a tarnished kettle to issue clouds of steam. She was young, slim and, even while seated, seemed to be tall in stature. Through the glasses he could see the wisps of hair, which had escaped the bun at the back of her neck, play around her forehead and cheeks in the breeze. She lifted one hand from the cover of the book in order to turn a page. "My God," Patrick whispered as the title was revealed – *The Ring and the Book* by Robert Browning.

The lenses in Patrick's eyes and in his mind were wide open. The naturalist in him dissolved in the shadows. When the pursued thrush flew across the path of his glasses he completely ignored it. Instead, he watched the woman now with intense curiosity, scrutinizing the details of her dress, the rings on her slender hands, taking note of the lace on her collar, the gold band on her left hand. Mud on her boots and on the hem of her dress indicated that she had been climbing on the bank. The apron that partly covered the skirt suggested that she must have been occupied with some chore before deciding to come to that exact spot, before deciding to read. Patrick was mildly amused when he discovered that she was drinking tea and, even more so, when he noted that her cup and saucer were made of English bone china. She was, he decided, very beautiful, in an unusual way. Some strength there, in her face, in the way her body relaxed into the landscape – unafraid, unaware of the possibility of an intruder.

His legs were beginning to cramp but Patrick was afraid to move, lest he might disturb her, or worse, bring attention to himself. He began to examine the woods surrounding the woman with deep interest, as if her environment was an extension of herself. He found one area where the trees had been cleared and another where there was evidence of some sort of cultivation. There was a stump, also, carved into the shape of a large chair and on this rested a notebook and pen, a knife, a loaf of bread, and, most surprisingly, a vase filled with wildflowers. Near the edge of the bank there was some sort of man-made structure which consisted of planks and supports and which appeared to be, somehow, broken. He puzzled for a while over its possible use, then moved the lenses of the fieldglasses deeper into the forest on either side and behind the woman.

Patrick began to search for evidence of the man connected to the gold band which now, coincidentally, covered the word *Ring* on the book's cover. He looked past trees, down the line of the path which he knew led eventually to the road, and into the clear spaces that appear for no reason in otherwise full shrubs and bushes. He changed his position somewhat so that he could see a little way down the bank. The wind shifted and a low, steady noise reached him from the whirlpool.

He had never been down to the edge of the river. The wide-open lenses in his mind pictured the current for a few seconds. Suddenly he was absolutely sure that the woman was, at this moment, completely alone. He looked at her face through the glasses. Then he rose slowly to his feet and walked, very quietly, away.

II

Because she lived, worked, and slept in the same series of rooms, Maud was only dimly aware of the transitional seasons of spring and fall. When she was a child walking to school there had been crisp, dry leaves scraping across the gravel to make her notice autumn and, in spring, crocuses, their colours blazing against dirty snow. Now the less subtle seasons of summer and winter always came as a kind of shock to her when they eventually forced themselves upon her attention. Particularly early summer. The wind would change one day, would slide in through the slightly open window, and would remind her of all she had neglected; the garden, her husband's memory, her child. Then, quite suddenly, she would want to nurture, to cause each of these things to grow, an emotion most often associated with spring, the season she had been able to utterly ignore.

On this particular June morning Maud was walking aimlessly back and forth across the Oriental carpet that covered the sunroom floor. The sudden change in the wind, and what it had evoked, had made her restless, almost nervous, and she paused now and then to pick up small items and to rearrange them even though her attention was elsewhere and she did not fully understand what they were. She exchanged a silver vase with a china figurine on the chest of drawers and then, finding herself with the inexplicable vase in her hand, she placed it, for no reason, on the window-sill in the light. The reflected glare bouncing from the object in that setting left her, momentarily, almost blind. Then, as the dark shapes of the room's furniture came back into focus, she sat down on a large doily-covered armchair and surveyed her surroundings as if she had never really seen them before.

She realized, with mild astonishment, that the contents of this room, and of all the other rooms that led to and from this one, had, more often than not, been brought into her home by clients who had been unable to pay their accounts at some time or another over the period of the last sixty years. Each chair, each table, each sofa, therefore, called to mind a funeral, or part of a funeral and, in most cases, represented much more than the funeral in question was worth. The piano, for instance, recalled the burial of one of the town mayors; a greedy, vain little man whose brief tenure in power had gone entirely to his head, causing him to croak out the desire for a large, showy funeral just before he died of apoplexy brought about by a heated argument at a town council meeting. Even during business hours when she was absolutely unable to play it, Maud loved the piano as much as she had detested the thoroughly tin-eared mayor, and so now looked upon the instrument's presence in her parlour as the result of miraculous circumstances. There it stood, so calm, so monumental, discreetly keeping its potential for music intact during times of silence.

Six years before, when she was newly married, the periods of enforced quiet had disturbed Maud – times when she had sat dutifully over some senseless piece of embroidery while downstairs mourners had recited measurements for coffins. It had been as if, in her own life, emotion had been held in suspense, so that the rest of the world could live and love and, more importantly, die. So the rest of them could respond while she worked garlands of flowers onto a piece of unbleached cotton and her young husband presided over the ritual in progress at the most recently bereaved household. She and her mother-in-law sitting there in the parlour, noiselessly drinking tea, waiting for a long thin line of mourners to appear in the graveyard outside the window; the signal that another funeral was finished, that the men would soon climb the stairs and life, as the women knew it then, would begin again.

Today, however, there was no one but herself; no funeral to be thought about and worried over, no casket to be hurriedly constructed. Not that it would have bothered her had things been otherwise. She had quickly become familiar with the ever-present corpse and the ever-present sorrow that accompanied it. She had become familiar with the oddities of the business; the cumbersome equipment of the embalming room, the display room with its mahogany and pine boxes, the children's hearse in the stable, the black plumes for the horses' heads which hung on the interior walls of that building like successfully hunted birds. All this seemed no more charged with meaning for her now than the incidents of the rest of her daily life. Now when she saw the children's hearse being prepared with white flowers and pansies from the garden, on the occasions when she was unable to complete the task herself, she no longer turned her face away from it as she had in the past. Instead, she checked to see that the work was satisfactory; that it was a fitting vehicle for one of the little dead children she invariably became so attached to.

In many ways she thought the little pony-drawn wagon resembled the coaches she had seen in Toronto on merry-go-rounds of that variety. And once, it had occurred to her that it looked suspiciously like a wedding cake.

The business and the house that Maud had married into stood practically dead centre on Main Street, flanked by a green-grocer on one side and a bakery on the other. Grady and

Son occupied a large frame building, plain in appearance and painted a neutral shade of grey with white trim around the windows and underneath the eaves. Its façade was neither elegant nor shabby, reflecting the taste and commonsense of the first Drummondville Grady who had constructed it shortly after his patriotic trek from Pennsylvania to Canada at the beginning of the century. With him, he had brought his family, a small amount of cash, a tattered and cherished Union Jack, and the tools of his trade: clamps, drills, nails, planers. He was a cabinetmaker. He soon discovered, however, that in the small pioneer settlement where he had chosen to spend the rest of his life, very few could afford mahogany and velvet and that there was much more call for simple pine boxes than for octagonal tea tables. A practical man, and one who had a family to feed, he adjusted, accepted his fate, and became the local undertaker, saving his more creative work for those times when, inexplicably, the steady flow of deaths abated for a while.

As the century progressed and the business of burying humans became more complex, several additions were tacked on to the original building. The population of the surrounding villages increased until the entire area became a sizeable town called Niagara Falls, not to be confused with the town on the lake which was also called Niagara. Now there were professionals living there who not only wanted, but could also afford, mahogany and velvet. But the second and third Grady did not construct tea tables and used these materials only in their more expensive caskets. The business prospered.

All of the Mrs. Gradys occupied themselves with arranging and rearranging the half-acre of land behind the frame building that housed, not only the business, but their living quarters as well. They planted bulbs, trimmed rose bushes, installed arbours and miniature artificial waterways. They gave little thought to the fact that the land they worked was rich with recent history, the Battle of Lundy's Lane having been fought where the garden was now and in the orchard and cemetery adjacent to it. Occasionally, they would unearth a bullet or a button, which they would place in an apron pocket where it would lie forgotten until it was thrown in the trash by the housekeeper at wash time. More excitement was caused by the discovery of cannon-balls, which were taken into the stables by the men, scrubbed and kept, although, until the military historian at the hotel across the street became interested, no one quite knew why.

Main Street was situated far enough up the hill from the river to be spared any of the garish tourist attractions that dominated the lower town and so, in appearance, it resembled the principal thoroughfare of any other Southern Ontario settlement of a similar size. Its inhabitants, therefore, were able to ignore the presence of the giant waterfall in a way the rest of the world seemed unable to. They were familiar enough with its existence that it aroused in them absolutely no curiosity, and they were too far away from it to use it to their financial advantage. The spray and fog which in winter caused the trees closer to the river to be covered with ice, producing a totally altered landscape, did not reach as far as Main Street. Even the roar of the cataract (which was never as loud as it was purported to be) was very rarely heard. Only on exceptionally still, exceptionally cold nights, when all motion had stopped or was frozen, buried, or asleep – only then could you hear it. And then it sounded like the ghost of some battle, so distant, so forgotten, that the rhythms of the cannon fire were practically lost.

Forgotten history, buried bullets; a long, even breath of noise, an incessant sigh, rubbing against the night.

Her abrupt awareness of the season had moved Maud over to the windows. She was gazing down at a small mud puddle watching the sun perform inside it like quicksilver. Touched by the wind the fiery ball became fragmented there, broken into piercing shards. Maud closed her eyes. The shards remained, fractured, in her mind's eye. But the puddle was gone.

Outside, a trolley approached and moved on. The clock on the mantel ticked. A rectangle of sun on the carpet crept a fraction of an inch closer to the wall.

Down the hall Maud could hear the housekeeper speaking to the child, dressing him for an outing. "Now you can put on your coat," she was saying encouragingly. "You can do it all by yourself."

No, thought Maud, he can't. He can't do anything all by himself. Anger flickered for a moment in her nervous system, like the sun in the puddle, then it drifted away.

"Now, let me tie your hat," the housekeeper was saying.

Maud heard their footsteps move down the hall towards the stairs. The stairs would take a long time, she knew. The child stiff-legged, unco-operative, responding neither to coaxing nor command. She looked across the room to the account book which lay open, unfinished, on the desk. She could faintly hear the footsteps of the men in another part of the house, and then some others, unfamiliar. Going to the display room, she thought vaguely. Sweet Repose, Journey's End, Gone Before, she murmured, reciting the familiar names of the various coffins.

She should be cutting roses in the garden, placing them in bowls of water in her dining room and parlour, filling her rooms with seasonal explosions of dark colour. She should at least be weeding the rock garden.

The crunch of wagon wheels on the gravel below the north windows of the sunroom. Maud recognized immediately the approach of the vehicle that picked up lifeless bodies; the meat wagon, as her husband had called it when he was speaking with the men.

She walked to the opposite side of the room and looked down. The men were opening the vehicle's back doors. When, instead of the usual wicker basket, they pulled out a galvanized sealed box shaped like a casket but of perfectly rectangular proportions, Maud brought her right hand, now suddenly cold, up against the warmth of her neck.

The ice in the river had broken up months ago, had moved downstream and disappeared. The whirlpool had resumed its circular journey. The upper rapids, the lower rapids, had resumed their own special dance of death. The Falls were, as usual, magnificent. Once the river shook off winter, separating into its moods and sequential performances, people began to drown themselves in it, sometimes accidentally, more often not. And the Old River Man, down by the whirlpool, fishing for his ghastly catch at a bottle a find; Maud's subsequent job ... the endless, futile attempts at identification which disturbed and frustrated her.

Part of the business she now owned. Spring and summer at Grady and Son. Dark roses and drowned flesh.

She searched the several cubbyholes of the rolltop desk for the small book where she kept the information. It didn't take her long to find it, and once she had, she discovered that the gum label which had adorned the leather cover had, for some reason, disappeared over the winter. Now, like almost everything described inside it, the book itself was unidentified. She opened one of the small drawers at the upper left of the desk and, moving aside a mass of paper clips, she pulled out a packet of gum-backed labels, edged in red. Licking one, she fixed it to the book's brown cover with two determined thumps of her right fist. Then, dipping her pen in the well, she wrote: *Description of Bodies Found in the Niagara River, Whirlpool, etc., 1887 –*

It was unnecessary to furnish the final date. A smaller document than the battleground that Grady and Son stood upon, its history was not finished. The book was not yet full.

II

In one sense the whirlpool was like memory; like obsession connected to memory, like history that stayed in one spot, moving nowhere and endlessly repeating itself. Above it, stars that appeared stationary traced their path across the sky, actually going somewhere, changing.

Fleda was outside the tent. Behind her it glowed in the night like a mystical pyramid. Around her, the unidentifiable night sounds; two million species of insects competing for pitch, volume, and space. Fleda stirring water in the last embers of the fire, extinguishing it.

Inside the tent, separated from her by only a thin piece of fabric, was her husband who, at this moment, had had just about enough of the Siege of Fort Erie. The armies in his mind had attacked and counter-attacked for three hours now until he could barely remember what they had been fighting for. The vague anger that he had felt towards the American Regiments when he had sat down to write had been replaced by boredom. Often, when he was working on his battle histories he could actually feel the regimental energy flow from his pen, almost as if he, himself, were inventing the plan of attack. Tonight, however, working for the first time in the tent, he was easily distracted, unable to maintain the concentration level necessary to sort through the thousands of details of the event.

He pushed back his chair and turned to look at his wife who, last time he noticed, had been reading in the wicker rocker just in front of the mosquito netting that led to the outdoors. He had wanted her to put down her book, to speak to him, to break his ennui. But where the devil had she got to?

"Fleda-a-a!" he bellowed in a voice he found most effective when shouting orders at a platoon of men marching half a mile away.

She appeared instantly, flung aside the mosquito netting, collapsed in her wicker chair, and picked up her book.

"Fleda," he began again, his mouth relaxing amiably under the weight of his walrus moustache, "Fleda, I'm bored."

"Absolutely not," she replied, "and besides the dress isn't here."

"You didn't bring the dress?"

"No."

"Why on earth not?"

"Because I left it at the hotel." She shifted in her chair, turned a page of the book. "Besides, I'm bored with that outfit. If you want to play dress-up with me, why not something a little more glamorous? It doesn't take long for a muddy calico dress to become boring. Why not silk or velvet? The whole thing makes me decidedly uncomfortable. I hate the way you look at me in that dress."

"But why, for heaven's sake, it's simply research ... you know it's the subject of my next paper."

"So that explains why every time you want me to dress up as Laura Secord you get that look on and say" – this in a whining voice imitating his own – "'*Fleda, I'm bored*.'" She finally looked up from her book. "Did it ever occur to you," she asked him, "that you married me precisely and only because, in some odd way, I remind you of Laura Secord?"

Major David McDougal laughed good-naturedly. "Don't be ridiculous," he said, without a great deal of conviction.

"No, really, it could be absolutely true." She moved the idea around in her mind for a few moments and then sat bolt upright in her chair.

"That's really insulting, you know," she continued, "marrying me for a reason like that. For all I know she may have been hideous, she may have had no front teeth, she may have weighed more than her cow."

Now, Major David McDougal roared with laughter. His wife was cheering him up, there was no doubt of that. He decided to pursue the subject further.

"How tall would you say she might have been? A giantess perhaps?" McDougal seemed to like this idea. "How about an amazon ... perfectly proportioned, but huge. Imagine the breasts! No wonder the Indians didn't attack her!"

"Maybe she was prematurely old, wrinkled, and grey." Fleda turned to her husband and continued wickedly. "Or maybe ... she was fraternizing with the American officers. Did you ever think of that?"

"Impossible!"

"Why?"

"Far too patriotic."

"Maybe she did it for patriotic reasons ... or," Fleda smiled innocently at David, "maybe she tried to fraternize with them and failed as a result of her awful appearance. Then her heroic act would be merely the revenge of a woman scorned. Remember, her husband was wounded."

"Do you want to know what I really think?" David asked, moving over to the bed at the far end of the tent. "I always thought, and I still do, that Laura was loyal, strong, and very beautiful." He lay back on the bed and rested his head on his hands behind him. Then he looked at his wife teasingly. "I always imagined her arriving at Fitzgibbon's headquarters, flushed and panting, her hair in a state of lovely disarray."

"She's the only woman in the whole story, so you simply romanticize her to *death*! Really, David."

"No more than Patmore romanticizes his precious angel

in his precious house. As for the celebrated Mr. Browning ... need I even comment?"

"Leave Browning out of this ... and as for Patmore ... you gave me that book. Besides, it's poetry."

"Aha!" McDougal pounced on his wife's last statement. "So what we are saying is that we may romanticize poetic women but not historical women, is that it ... is that what we are saying?"

"Well, it seems the proper thing to do, if you must romanticize your women at all ... the Lovely Elaine, the Lady of Shallot."

"Yes, but supposing those ladies are historical as well as poetic ... then the historical would have to come first. Though, I must say, I do have trouble believing that Patmore's wife ever existed ... that she was anything more than a figment of his imagination. Didn't she conveniently die?"

"Yes, but you can hardly blame Patmore for that."

"Oh, I don't know, it must be uphill work being an angel, especially in a poet's house. Maybe she died of ennui." Fleda scowled at him. He eyed her closely. "Who would you rather be, if you had a choice, Patmore's wife or Laura Secord?"

"Since it seems very unlikely that I shall have the opportunity to be either, I find that question impossible to answer. The Americans are quite well-behaved these days, there is absolutely no point reporting their activities to the military hereabouts."

McDougal interjected at this point. This was a subject on which he had very definite and serious opinions. "Don't be so sure," he muttered darkly. "Don't be so bloody sure."

"As for Patmore's wife," Fleda gestured to the canvas walls around her, "I have no house to be an angel in."

"You'll have your house, but you still haven't told me which you'd rather be, if you had the choice."

"Patmore's wife, I suppose, even if she is dead. I would love to have my portrait painted by Rossetti. And the book, imagine having your husband write a book for you."

"I will write a book on Laura Secord and pattern her character on yours."

"Really, David, I doubt that she and I would have a single thing in common." Fleda left her chair and moved over to the bed, willing now to take part to a certain extent in the game. "Supposing she wasn't like me at all, not a single bit?"

"Well, I imagine her looking exactly like you, but wilder and in greater disarray, of course, after her valorous trek through the woods." McDougal pulled his wife down beside him on the bed and said, "Then I imagine that Fitzgibbon would be strangely moved by her appearance."

Major McDougal was beginning to undress.

"David . . ."

"Then I imagine," he said, leaving his clothes in an untidy pile on the floor and climbing under the blankets, "that Fitzgibbon would dismiss his colleagues so that he could speak to Laura alone . . . confidential military information and all that. Then I imagine. . ." he began to undo the small buttons on the front of her dress. "Then I imagine . . . ."

"David . . . just a moment."

"Mmmm?" he said, biting her ear.

"You are overlooking a very important fact."

"What's that?" he asked, reaching up under her long skirt and pressing his face against her neck.

"Laura Secord was a married woman."

"So are you," he replied, leaning outwards from the bed in order to extinguish the coal-oil lamp.

He made love, for all his kindness, like a man fighting a short, intense battle, a battle that he always won. She lay passively beneath him like a town surprised by an invasion of enemy troops. Afterwards, he fell asleep almost immediately, like a man overcome by battle fatigue.

She crept across the tent, after, to find her long white

nightgown with its high neck and lace cuffs. Then she walked outside, barefoot in the cold, wet grass, down the path to the bank. She could see the whirlpool from there and, further away, the rapids in the moonlight. She knew that she had lied. She wouldn't ever want to be Patmore's wife, Patmore's angel. Not now, not ever.

⁊

The next time Patrick entered the woods above the whirlpool he was prepared and unencumbered. He had left his bird dictionary and his wildflower book on a small wooden table at the farm. He had dressed in browns and greens for the purpose of camouflage. He had snuck through the orchards like a deserter, his fieldglasses bumping quietly against his ribs.

He was sure she would be there.

The previous days had been overcast, wet, hardly weather to be reading Browning in the woods. Yet somehow, Patrick could not imagine this woman occupying rooms. He believed she would have remained throughout the downpour, hardly moving except to turn the pages of her book. Patrick had stayed indoors, watching the fog in the orchard through the window and also reading Browning, as if in preparation.

At night he dreamed of faceless women, shadows of leaves moving on their white skin.

He was sure she would be there and rejected any possibility that she might have been a transient, a traveller, one who could have paused in that spot merely to catch her breath ... for a rest. Something in her posture suggested permanence. The woods were easy with her. And she would be there. He knew it.

Until that moment a week earlier, it had never occurred

to him that a figure would enter any of his landscapes. They were fierce places, wild with growth, crazy with weather. Places where, a hundred miles north, huge fires ate their way through darkness while animals ran helplessly before them. Patrick feared the fires though he knew they rarely travelled this far south. He feared them and dreamed them, imagining the inside of his rooms turning orange.

The fires, he supposed, had never made an appearance on this woman's mind.

Once, when he was a child, a neighbouring barn had burned in winter, melting the snow for yards around. He would always remember the heat of that fire on his face and the cold and the cast of the fire on the faces around him.

Terrifying.

This woman's face was cool, absorbed.

Now as Patrick crossed the car tracks at the edge of the woods he was pleased to see that the rain had brought the foliage out to such an extent that it created a solid mesh of light green. This screen would perfect his camouflage.

Once he stepped onto the path he began to move in the manner of Indians, checking the ground for fallen twigs and avoiding them, performing a sort of silent, drunken dance. He was amazed to find himself in a set of circumstances where even the snap of a twig might alter everything utterly. Normally, landscape seemed too large for him to have any effect at all upon his surroundings. Now, detail drew him in, connecting him with the earth beneath him. The floor of the woods became an obstacle course, cluttered with natural traps that could result in error.

He recognized the spot he was searching for by the familiar sumac bush and a small, unhealthy cedar that looked as if it couldn't decide whether to grow beyond shrubhood. Crouching down behind the latter, and adjusting himself to the most comfortable hidden position, he brought the glasses up to his eyes and focused them on the correct location.

No woman.

Patrick was dumbfounded. He *knew* she would be there. How could this portion of the forest exist were she not in it? He wanted to start all over again; to walk out the door, over the orchards, through the woods, to approach this spot one more time. As if there had been a mistake in his route that he could now correct. He would do it all over again, right to the moment of lifting his glasses to his eyes. Then she would be there. He searched again. Still no woman. Just lime green woods and several birds whose identities, at this moment, didn't interest him in the least.

Still no woman. Sick with disappointment and self-doubt, he wanted to turn and leave the place. He felt cheated – as if the woman had made him a promise that she had never intended to keep. He would turn and leave the place. He would never come back, never see her again. He would never again allow a figure to enter his landscapes. He was perspiring with the utter futility of it all.

Then a sudden movement in the bushes near the bank. Instinctively he searched for a bird. A thin, high sound moved through the woods. Singing. And then the woman's face, followed by her blue dress, emerging from the other side of the bank.

Patrick froze. He was now standing, unprotected by greenery, and she was coming closer and closer. Very, very slowly he returned to the crouching position. He was afraid that she might hear his heart which seemed to have moved from its normal location in order to pound, disturbingly, in his brain. She was so near now that there was no need for the glasses. His inclination was to bolt, run right out of the woods, back to the farm, onto a train. Vacate the province. Leave the country.

But he couldn't move. At this moment his eyes were less than two feet away from her blue skirt, which for some crazy reason he now noticed was wrinkled, and covered with spots of mud. She's been reading, he thought, and the mud comes from the bank.

The sound of pouring water. Objects he had previously overlooked came into focus: a wash-tub vaguely in the middle distance, and a barrel, not three feet away from him, probably for collecting water. He remembered the tea.

She was now using a dipper, pouring water from the barrel into a galvanized pail. He heard the pot scrape against the edge of the wood and then the luxurious sound of water falling and connecting with liquid already in the pail.

The sound soothed him. He knew she would not see him now, now that she was absorbed in this activity. He relaxed, listening to the rhythm of the task. Dip, pour . . . dip, pour. Her skirt moving in front of him like a heavy curtain in the wind, as she leaned forward to scoop the water out of the barrel, and then sideways to pour it into the pail.

When she was finished, she bent to lift the pail and walked, straight-backed, away from him, the weight that she carried never once interfering with the level line of her shoulders. Then, as she moved into the distance, he watched that level tilt to the left as she poured the liquid from the pail into a large pot which hung over the makeshift fireplace. Several dishes were scattered around this location; cups, plates, saucers and cutlery gleaming in the sun.

Suddenly he understood. Breakfast. A domestic event had taken place very near the spot where he had first sighted her. This water was for washing up. She would begin, once the water was warm, to wash the dishes, like an ordinary woman. As if there had been walls around her, and furniture.

Patrick lifted the glasses and focused on her face. He wanted to see if he could tell by a change in her expression, the exact moment when the water began to boil.

✸

Fleda, breathing heavily because of the long, steep climb, returned from the whirlpool late in the morning. At the top of the bank she leaned her back against a fir tree which grew out at an angle over the drop. She could feel the roughness of the bark push its way through her cotton clothing, and with one hand she absently caressed this uneven texture while she waited for her heartbeat to return to normal. When it did, she placed her two palms against the tree behind her and levered herself into an upright standing position. Then she walked over to the tent to search for her diary.

David had repaired the makeshift desk at the edge of the bank so Fleda, journal now in hand, headed in its direction. When she arrived she pulled up a suitable stump, fastidiously removed one or two bird droppings from her workplace, and placed the notebook on the weathered planks. Taking a pencil from her pocket she began to write.

25 June 1889

Every day when David leaves, either for the camp or for the rooms in town, I go down to the whirlpool.

All by myself at the water's edge I make small boats out of folded birch bark and then I push them out into the current.

This takes most of the morning.

Little white vessels departing from the shore, set adrift on a long tour of the whirlpool. Like people, just like people. A complete revolution would be a long, long life. Not many are able to go the distance. Those that do I am unsure of. Have they moved around the full circumference or have they doubled back somehow on an unknown current? Have they been affected by wind? I have begun to mark my boats in some way, making each one different from the others. And I have begun to give them names, like real ships. "Adonais," "Dreamhouse," "Warrior," "Angel."

With a pencil from my apron pocket I write the words on the birch bark in clear block letters. Then I launch my small craft from the shore and pick up Browning in order to read while I wait for them to return.

Yesterday, the Old River Man passed by and I spoke to him but he didn't answer. He walks around the edge of the whirlpool as if he is looking for something among the stones, even pushes his walking stick into the tall grass that grows beyond them. He seems, at these times, to be completely ignoring the water. I think I understand this.

He knows the water. There is hardly anything that he doesn't know about the water. He knows the whole river. He can't live in the water but he lives as close to it as he can. But he has to be careful. The land is something he will never entirely learn, so, for him, each step there is investigative, an exploration. He won't ever speak to me because I belong to the land, which is what I know. For me, the water is dangerous. I suppose I'll never really understand it. So I study it. He stands at the very edge of the water and looks at that land which, for him, is as unfathomable as the whirlpool is to me, as undecipherable as the upper and lower rapids.

People are always building houses out of the materials they know so that they can crawl inside and think about the

materials that they don't. The River Man lives beside the
water, which is safe for him and he thinks about dry rocks,
sand, grasses, trees, cliffs, hills, fields. He can't kill in a
territory he doesn't understand, so he doesn't hunt, he
fishes. Everything he swallows is either made of water or
comes from the water. It is his survival.

I am surrounded by grasses, trees, earth. Everything I
eat grows on the land, but I think about the water all the
time. It is constantly on my mind.

My games are played with small, benign toys. Today
"Warrior" came in first, followed shortly thereafter by
"Adonais" and "Dreamhouse."

Fleda lifted her head and tightened the muscles in her neck,
shoulders, and back. In this alert posture she resembled a
small animal who was trying to ascertain the level of danger
in a distant, barely discernible sound.

In fact she was not listening to, or for, anything; had
merely startled herself by what she had written.

The little boat, "Angel," had not returned, or if it had,
she had completely failed to notice it.

❦

◊ Late in the afternoon, Maud Grady decided to take the child out for a stroll in the garden. Downstairs, at the back of the house, the workshops were silent, the men having left over an hour ago to preside over a procession and interment.

She had spent the better part of the afternoon with the child, this being the housekeeper's day off, and had tried repeatedly to capture his attention. It was no use, however. Regardless of her actions, of the brightly coloured objects that she dangled before him, he remained bent over a small toy rabbit, now almost lacking in woollen fur, stroking it rhythmically. Finally, emotionally drained by the effort, she collapsed in the armchair with the *Ladies' Home Journal* and grimly waited out the rest of the afternoon. Until this moment when she decided that they both might benefit from some fresh air.

They left the building by a side door situated closer to the street than to the garden and began to walk along the edge of the house. The child, still clutching the rabbit in his free hand, walked in a stiff-legged fashion like one whose limbs have been confined to braces for a great deal of time and who is only now beginning, once again, to be mobile. His eyes remained lowered as though he were concentrating on each footstep. But a closer examination of his line of vision would have revealed a fixed scrutiny of the ground before him, rather than his shoes.

Everything about him was locked into a stiff, unbreakable pose: the unchanging angle of his stare, his straight knees, the hand which his mother held, the fingers which refused to grasp. Only the area of his body directly surrounding the toy rabbit was soft and unmechanical. There, his fingers curled into the remaining plush and his elbow and shoulder bent to harbour and protect.

Halfway along the outer wall of the building they passed a screen door, the wooden frame of which was painted white to match the trim of the rest of the building. Partially blinded by the sun in front of her, Maud was able to make out only a single gas light behind it and the odd hulking form of a partially constructed coffin. Before he had been called into duty, the carpenter had obviously been at work on yet another casket. Maud's exertions with the child earlier in the afternoon had left her so exhausted that she could not now muster curiosity enough to wonder whether or not there had been a purchaser for this item. Business, for once, was not occupying her thoughts.

Still holding the child's hand, she entered the garden and looked past the grass and rockery and flowers, down to the end of the property where several tall beech trees threw shadows so long they almost reached her feet. Between these, and trapped in their early summer leaves, was an intense, copper wealth of sunlight which had so transformed the contents of the garden that each shrub, each flower, appeared to be illuminated from within. Even the wire and wooden fence at the back stood altered; magnificent, its surfaces etched and clear, while in the vegetable patch directly in front of it, humble early lettuce assumed the grace of great sculpture. Beyond her own property, Maud could see the stones of Drummond Hill Cemetery glowing like white teeth on the horizon.

Unexpectedly, she was filled with awe for this small world

which included only that which she could see – this landscape of garden and graveyard where no streetcar trespassed; filled with wonder that she had created some of it herself, caused, for instance, the grape arbour to exist on the left side of the garden, the roses to decorate the centre. Even the grass, each blade of which was now standing as sharp as the cutting instrument for which it was named, had been coaxed into lushness by her diligence concerning the removal of weeds.

The child had removed his hand from hers and was, once again, engaged in stroking the rabbit, over and over, as he stood silently at her side. Maud looked down at the top of his head which almost reached her waist. She noticed he was beginning to rock slightly as he caressed his toy.

"Gar-den," she said to him slowly, moving her hand at the end of her arm with the palm turned upwards, back and forth across the lot behind the house. "Ga-a-a-r-den."

The child gave no indication that he was aware she was speaking to him.

Maud sighed and, taking the child's hand again, she led him over to the area of the garden which was filled with rocks and the small plants that people habitually place in such a locality – miniature shrubs of unnatural shades and textures, tiny rubbery leaves of grey or white, or scratchy purplish growths that seemed to be formed of sands and gravels. The rocks themselves looked as if they had been magically transported from another planet, formed out of substances quite foreign to the earth. Or as if they had been frozen in the process of a strange evolution which left them filled with holes and bubbles. In order to break the odd moon-like surface of this portion of the garden, Maud had planted some tulip bulbs the previous fall and now at the end of their season, they had dropped some of their petals into the rockery. The intense, raking light caused these small pools of colour to blaze there and the rock garden, in contrast, to appear even more ominous than before. Maud had a brief childish fantasy about being an insect in such a landscape.

She multiplied the size of each plant while walking through a jungle of them towards the still sea of the fish pond. This was to remain empty of fish, filled with leaves and algae, until the end of June.

The child, she knew, would respond to the fish, if she were to take him into the heated carriage house where they were kept for all but two months of the year. He would stand stiff-legged with his hands against the glass tank. He would watch them move around and around in the gloom.

She remembered the time he had disappeared for an afternoon, how the entire household had been raised into a frantic search, how it had been she, herself, who had finally found him, standing perfectly still in the carriage house, watching the fish in their long tank, the only light in the place coming from one small, dirty window. The coffins stored all around the tank made it seem to be just another model of the species, its rectangular shape as regular as the others. As she approached him, she realized that the child could see the reflection of his own face on the wall of glass in front of him. The fish, the bubbles, were like the thoughts that moved back and forth through the liquid of his untouchable mind.

Now she scraped her boot over the stone in front of her. "Rock," she said, half-heartedly, not really expecting a reaction. She reached forward and gently pulled the dying blossom of a red tulip closer to the child's face. "Flower," she said.

This absurd naming of objects had become one of the rituals of the day. When Maud ate breakfast with the child while he was being fed by the housekeeper, she found that she automatically identified each object that she held in her hand. "Spoon," she would say, just before she placed it in her mouth. "Coffee, cup, bread, jam, butter, milk. . . ." Then it was a calm methodical exercise, requiring little effort, something that had entered the realm of habit. But now, no longer confined by walls where the number of objects to name is finite, the enormity of the task confounded her.

"Tree," she said loudly, to no one in particular, as if the child were not there at all. "Fence, sky, cloud, grass, watering can, spade." Then, reckless in the face of the futility of it all, she began to shout in anger the names of objects and entities that were not there. "Snow, train, desert, ocean, dog, shopping bag, roast beef, plum pudding, mop, lamp!"

The child had returned to the rabbit and was now focused on one of its ears, which he rubbed softly with two of his stiff fingers.

For a brief moment, Maud stood outside herself and witnessed her own performance – a young woman standing in a garden with a totally unresponsive child, shouting nonsense into the air. Her first inclination was to be amused. But the heat of the sun on her back reminded her of the heat of her anger ... directed now towards the child, his unwillingness, his refusals, his total withdrawal. He was like an invisible wall that she ran into daily, bruising herself with each contact, until the very knowledge of its existence brought her only a memory of pain. And anger in the presence of pain.

Suddenly this anger spilled out of Maud's heart and into her body, adrenalin rushing like fire through her veins. Turning around with one whirling gesture, she grabbed the child by the hair. Now they were facing directly into the sun and Maud became blinded, both by its strength and the strength of her own emotion. With her fist in his hair and her other hand under his chin, she jerked the child's face up from its downcast attitude. As he began to struggle, he dropped the toy rabbit into the grim landscape of the rock garden. Maud pulled his small body closer to her, firmly securing his hips between her knees, keeping a strong grip on his hair, his face, as he squirmed and his stiff arms flailed in a struggle to escape. With her elbows she pinned his upper arms to his body. She could feel the fear in his chest, practically hear the thrashing of his heart. Amazed at her own strength, she moved two of her fingers down from his scalp and peeled back one of his eyelids. Then she screamed the word "SUN!" directly into his left ear.

Everything about the small creature that she held was in a state of explosive, violent withdrawal. "SUN!" she screamed again, looking, herself, right into the centre of the burning orb, allowing the pain of this vision to penetrate behind her eyes. She forced the child's eyelid further open, noticing that the other eye was completely, stubbornly sealed. She roughly adjusted once again the angle of his face.

"SUN!" she shrieked. "SUN, SUN, SUN, SUN!!"

A desperate, rusty sound began to issue from the child's mouth, which, until this moment, had been frozen into the shape of a silent howl. The noise was that of a hoarse cry to which, at first, Maud paid no attention. Then slowly, her fury subsiding, she perceived that his small body had relaxed in her grip and was now convulsing. From his lips came an almost unidentifiable sound, more like the moan or low growl of a terrified cornered animal than anything human.

"S-a-a-a-w-n," he groaned, followed by a long, slow, sob. "Sa-a-a-w-n!"

In astonishment, Maud let go of him and as she did, the other eye opened and the child took in all of the light. The sobs shook his entire body. Still he did not remove his eyes from the horizon which was filled with an agonizing radiance.

"S-a-a-awn!" he roared, unlocked now, stamping his feet on the grass, pounding his hips with his small fists. "S-a-a-w-n, s-a-a-a-w-n!"

Maud placed her hands on his shaking shoulders and turned him gently away from the blinding fire.

That was his first word.

Those were his first tears.

ℐ

His uncle's farm was prosperous – a kind of miniature empire with large cathedral-like barns, and board and batten sheds, and even a gazebo in the landscaped backyard. It consisted of land that had been forced into submission by several generations of large, heavy-muscled men with strong, obstinate wills. The house had been replaced three times in a century and now, at the farm's centre, and at the end of an impressive double row of sugar maples, there stood a seemingly indestructible fortress of red brick, entirely symmetrical, with windows and chimneys mirrored on either side of a Georgian door. Stretching out from this, in all directions, were acres and acres of fruit trees, each one pruned to size and irregular only in the grotesque gestures of their branches which were, in this season, disguised by a thick covering of leaves.

Patrick, arriving in this neat, well-ordered landscape, had felt, as always, his own sense of inadequacy and that of his father who, instead of taming the new land, had attempted to tame its inhabitants by preaching fire and brimstone sermons in poverty-stricken parishes. He taught his son how to read Latin instead of how to make a split rail fence and later spent the few dollars he was able to save having him properly educated, hoping that, when the process was complete, Patrick might decide to enter the ministry. The call had never come, however, and Patrick, unable to deal effectively with either the body or the soul of the new country, had found himself, at thirty-three, eking out a subsistence salary as a clerk in the capitol city, grasping desperately for bits of unstructured time in order to pursue his obsession with the art of poetry. And there was the disappointed wife who hovered in his mind as a constant reminder of his inability to provide, either physically or emotionally. Reading, always reading, she complained as night after night he disappeared into the old-world landscape with Wordsworth, Coleridge, or Browning.

In the beginning, his wife had accompanied him on his Sunday outings in the Gatineau Hills where he went in search of the often elusive inspiration. But eventually the cold and the boredom overcame her and the apparent futility of his quest. With the unexpected, practical intelligence that sometimes springs from those of uncomplicated mind, she had said to him one winter day as they stood surrounded by unvaried spruce, up to their hips in snow, "You're never going to find Wordsworth's daffodils here." After that, Patrick went into the woods alone.

He hated the cold, but clung to the concept of landscape and so he stubbornly persisted. With numb fingers he recorded his observations in his notebooks, waiting sometimes months until he moulded them into poems. Some of these had been published in one small magazine or another south of the border, and finally in a slim collection he had paid for himself. Just enough reinforcement to feed the disease, the desire; enough to make him believe that he was different from the men he worked with. Enough to ensure that he would stumble through each work day in a fog of utter loneliness.

During the past winter he had suffered an attack of pneumonia which had left him weaker physically and in a state of perpetual despair. He began to believe that there were forces beyond his control conspiring to erase all words from his mind. Finally, he found it difficult to speak at all.

The idea of people gathered together, the noise, the maddening hum of conversation, caused him panic. His doctor, genuinely alarmed, suggested a twelve-week vacation away from his work, the family, preferably in a rural setting. The uncle was contacted and generously opened the doors of his healthy world – a world that Patrick would feel, initially, overwhelmed by.

Within a few weeks, however, he would discover that his uncle was not particularly interested in whether or not his young nephew could build a barn or plough a furrow. In fact, he was much too busy to be concerned with him at all. And so Patrick was left alone to wander around the woods, birdwatching, collecting plant specimens, or simply allowing his mind to digest the scenery. He wrote no poems, having lost touch, somewhere during the illness, with that part of himself, but he slept a great deal and began to recover some of his lost weight.

He had visited this Niagara County farm often as a boy and so now he was able to behave there as one does with familiar people and places. He was able to choose either privacy or participation, depending on his mood. Most often he chose a combination of both, wanting the comfort of company without the responsibility for conversation or action attached to that comfort. He liked to listen to the mild, safe words which passed, in the evenings, between his uncle and aunt.

Two evenings before as he sat making notes in the parlour, thereby avoiding conversation, he had found himself listening to the old couple arguing a point. He could barely believe the coincidence.

"If I were interested in history," his uncle was saying, "I'd have no time for progress. I don't want to remember the way it was. All stumps and mud was the way that it was. What kind of a fool would want to remember that?"

"Well, the major's talks are learnèd," argued his aunt, "and he prints them up so that you can read afterwards what you don't understand."

"Don't tell me I don't understand. Any cow in the field understands stumps and mud."

"But this is the 1812 war he'll be talking about."

Patrick's uncle was unimpressed. "My grandfather fought in that war, lost the use of one arm, and was never given a stipend. It's nothing you'd want to remember. Let it go, that's my opinion."

"I'm going to the talk," his aunt insisted.

"Well, I'm not surprised. All the women for miles around will be filling up the hall because his own wife won't be there, and that's for sure."

"It's shameful," agreed Patrick's aunt, "her living in the woods out there, like a gypsy."

Patrick felt as if everything around him had suddenly jerked into focus.

"She should be having babies and minding house," his aunt continued.

"I've heard that the major's going to build her a house," said the uncle, "all made out of windows with – "

"I'll go with you, Aunt," Patrick interrupted from the other side of the room. His voice sounded unusually loud to him and oddly distant, as if someone else had shouted the sentence from a far corner of the house.

His aunt was pleased and surprised and began at once to direct her conversation towards her nephew: what she would wear; her friends and enemies who were likely to be there; the likelihood of the talk being too long; the suitability of the refreshments afterwards.

Patrick wasn't listening. He was trying to absorb the information that the woman in his mind had a flesh and blood husband. Something a little more tangible than the ring he had seen resting on the cover of the book.

Tonight he dressed for the lecture at the Historical Society with a certain sense of unease; more because of the anticipated crowd than because of the historian who fascinated him purely because he was married to the woman. History. Like his uncle, Patrick was confused by the word. History, his story, whose story? Collections of facts that were really only documented rumours. When he thought hard about them, thought hard about facts, they evaporated under his scrutiny. Crowds of men rushing towards each other with gleaming weapons. Fires. Large, hot, man-made fires. And the repetition. As if by speaking it over and over this collection of past facts might liquefy again, change from vapour into rain, become a large, touchable body of water.

He put on the same costume that he had worn in Ottawa, daily, to his place of employment. Dark jacket and pants. Dark vest, white shirt. He placed his pocket-watch, a silver circle with a locomotive etched on it, inside his vest pocket. That way, if necessary, he would be able to occupy himself by watching the progression of time.

One hour later he met the military historian.

"Major David McDougal," the large man introduced himself, pumping Patrick's hand vigorously. "So pleased to meet you. I've read some of your work ... in the Canadian Appendix to the *Younger American Poets*, I believe. Yes, I'm sure that's where it was. Very fine, very fine."

"Thank you," Patrick managed to croak, greatly surprised.

"We need writers!" the historian continued. "Yes, we need real writers ... thinkers. Yes, this country needs thinkers; thinkers that think Canadian. You *do* think Canadian, don't you?"

"Well, I hope ... I mean I think I think Canadian," Patrick replied, laughing.

"Good!" boomed McDougal emphatically, and without a hint of the other man's amusement. "Nobody else does. Thinking Canadian is a very lonely business, my boy, and don't forget it. Do they think Canadian at the University of Toronto? No, they don't. They think Britain ... the Empire and all that nonsense. Do they think Canadian in the churches? No, they don't. They think Scotland, Rome. Why not a church of Canada, I ask you? Surely we could at least have our own religion. I'll bet this group assembled here doesn't have more than one Canadian thought a day, and they pretend to be interested in Canadian history!" The major threw his arms straight up in the air in a gesture of bewildered outrage.

Throughout the long, well-researched, but undeniably boring lecture, Patrick did his best to appear as if he were thinking Canadian. He was oddly drawn to the speaker, liked his good-humoured, outspoken sense of betrayal, his unaffected pomposity. The poet's mind, however, tended to slip back into the woods above the whirlpool where he supposed the trilliums were about to disappear for the season. Soon the more colourful wildflowers of early July would replace them. He thought about the woman. He was sure she would still be reading, reading by moonlight, rising only to pour water into the kettle, the fire underneath it stronger in the dark. Occasionally, the major's voice broke into this picture and then Patrick looked through the windows of the hall into the night where he imagined the glow of battle fire on the surrounding orchards.

"So, you will come to visit me, I hope," the major said afterwards to Patrick. "In my rooms at the hotel I have incontestable proof that we won that battle regardless of what any American might try to tell you. Why all this running away, why all this casting of baggage into the river, I ask you? Why all this destroying of ammunition? Is that the way a victorious army behaves? Of course not!" The major snorted contemptuously.

"We won. There is simply no doubt about it. We fought hard, many, many lives were sacrificed ... but we won. Imagine having a victory stolen from you like that. The Americans are robbing us of our victories! It's unconscionable!"

Major McDougal was silent for a few moments, considering

The child was watching the fish in the pond, thinking that he would not stop, now that he had begun.

He wanted to move the fish around, to remove them from their various prisons, to interrupt their monotonous, seasonal journey from pool to tank and back again.

Why should they not have the rest of the garden, the rest of the world?

Why should they not have the dangerous sun as well as the soft, warm water?

The word *pool* spread over the child's brain, soft fins at his temples and then as an echo and then as a spiral.

When he hit the surface of the water with his palm, the fish moved in a jerky, hysterical fashion, turning sharp corners, their paths becoming rectilinear.

Gone the gentle undulations, the swishing of membrane through liquid. Enter the straight paths and intersections of fear.

The child looked at the drops of water on his palm. Suns in every bead of it and colours non-existent in the world.

The word *world* moved lazily behind his forehead, followed by the word *water*. And the word *weep* was in there too, trying to come forward.

His mother was working on the other side of the garden. Mud on her shoes, canvas gloves covering her hands. Digging to set in marigolds. Rust and yellow.

The child moved towards her, carrying a small burlap sack full of toy soldiers in one hand, his rabbit in the other. When he was near his mother he began to arrange the members of his tiny army in order of size, making a clucking noise that had nothing at all to do with soldiers. Perhaps, Maud speculated, the sound had something to do with horses. She would, she decided, buy him some toy horses. Hoping for the day when the syllables he spoke coincided with his activities.

By the time she had set in four plants he had moved away from the soldiers who remained behind in a rectangular block, perfectly organized upon the lawn. Maud paused to watch her child's progress across the yard, knowing that he would stop, once again, at the small rockbound pool.

He would stay there, more than likely, for the rest of the afternoon.

Pure sun today. Maud looked across the length of the property up the hill to the graveyard where the older stones gleamed from between clumps of cedars and the trunks of giant oaks. Not too much activity there. No funerals. A few widows perhaps, dragging yards of crape and carrying watering cans. This desperate desire to make something grow out of earth that held someone's bones. Maud kept her gardening close to the house, had not planted even a single geranium at the spot where Charles was buried, flanked by his parents. Pansies for her little friends in the children's hearse were more important. They had their own little garden right here.

She had visited Charles' grave only once; a strange, black-veiled creature she had been then, groping blindly from stone to stone, empty-handed, struggling along in her cocoon of crape. As she had expected, several spiders had made their webs between the marble columns on the front of the stone, from wingtip to wingtip of the angel that stood on top of it and in the grass adjacent. It had started to rain and, concerned about her already greying skin, Maud had hurried away from the spot, convinced that all was well there. She hoped to God that no over-zealous caretaker would decide to remove the webs, believing in her heart of hearts that the ground for miles around would shudder with Charles' wrath were that to take place. She thought also that, were it possible, she would have an entire sepulchre made for him from the webs of energetic spiders. An odd image this had produced in her imagination; a gauzy tent-like structure, festooned with wild, uncultivated roses, quivering in the breeze. More like the cradle of an enchanted princess than the grave of an ordinary undertaker.

Now, in her own garden, she began digging again with her little spade and within seconds struck something hard, unyielding. Subsequent attempts to budge the object produced the sound of metal against metal. Finally, she was able to slip the spade beneath the object's underside and lever it out of the ground to the side of the flower-bed where it rolled for a few inches before coming to a stop. Another cannon-ball. It left a smooth, spherical indentation in the earth where it had rested for some seventy-five years. Maud placed the roots of four or five marigolds there and quickly set the soil in around them. She would have one of the men come out to fetch the cannon-ball, put it in the barn with the others. She hadn't the least idea what ammunition such as this was meant to accomplish, whether it was meant to explode, to cause fire, or to shatter bones. Whatever the case, she would keep it for the military historian who lived in the hotel across the street. The one with the strange young wife who some said had gone to live in the woods alone. Maud, however, had seen her several times during the winter and so was inclined to discredit the story.

Patrick was standing ankle deep in the mallows at the shore watching, trying to understand the current of the whirlpool, throwing branches into the water, watching them move out into the width of the river, losing them, then finding them again, with the fieldglasses. The thing that confused him was the size, the breadth of the river here, so large that the bend in the current was practically invisible. Still the most complete stranger would be aware of the giant eddy, would speak the word "whirlpool." He knew that.

That morning he had begun a letter to his wife, attempting to describe this geography which she had never seen, attempting to describe his walks. He had surprised even himself by mentioning cliffs, waterfalls, orchards, woods, vineyards and whirlpools all in the same paragraph and he suspected that she would believe him to be romanticizing his surroundings. He told her he had stayed up until dawn after the lecture at the Historical Society thinking about the Battle of Lundy's Lane – the first time he had approached such a subject. Then, realizing that she would have little interest in either the landscape or the fighting, he had crumpled the paper in his fist.

He sat down on a rock near the shore and stared out over the water not wishing, as yet, to climb back up the bank. An otter appeared and slid into the water like a ghost without a backbone or a fish with fur.

This river was not the ocean, but it was staggering in the way he believed that the ocean might be. Its size, endless movement, shocked and moved him in a way that was basically silent. He had brought his notebook there, had the title "Maelstrom" on his mind, but no further words would come to him. It was like a conversation he couldn't begin, never mind finish, in some crazy way like talking to his wife in the moments of her silent anger when she seemed so much larger than him.

He remembered the smaller, more accessible lake where he had spent his childhood, remembered its details. He could, in fact, recall the bulrushes near the shore, how they bent in the wind and changed colour with the season. He knew how a slight shift of weather could change the surface of the lake, break apart its reflections. This water was untouchable, inexplicable. He felt he could really only see it from a distance, through a telescope, from another planet.

And then the sound of the rapids, camouflaging all danger. His childhood lake had magnified noise; in the winter or on still summer evenings you could hear coyotes move on the opposite shore, or the flap of a blackbird's wing sailing over the water to the forest.

Rice Lake, where the wild rice grew along the edges. Spook Island crouching offshore.

Once Patrick had been a swimmer in that shallow, gentle body of water. He would bathe with the Indian children from the reservation, gliding under water while they scrambled and splashed and pushed their bodies, churning through the surface, his fine hair trailing, reed-like behind him. Theirs pushed into irregular shapes by a fiercer combat with the water.

Submerge. To place oneself below and lose character, identity, inside another element. It was this quiet diving that attracted him, holding his breath for long periods, his eyes open, finally surprising himself when the weird landscape of Spook Island burst out at him when he surfaced.

There was never anything to see under there, the fine soil of the bottom clouding the water. Never anything to see but soft brown and shafts of sunlight penetrating this from the world above.

The world above. That's where he lived all the time now. Patrick had not swum for years. He remembered the liquid envelope, the feeling of total caress. Nothing but water and certain winds could touch him like that, all over.

It began to rain, large drops of water that were instantly swallowed by the whirlpool's restless surface. He collected some of them in the palm of his hand before the downpour thickened. When it did, he decided to begin the ascent to the top of the bank. After five minutes of hard climbing, he looked through the grey sheet of rain towards the summit. He was astonished to see the woman standing there under a black umbrella, apparently watching him. He began, once again, to climb, slipping now and then on the steep path which had become, almost immediately, unreliable with the change in the weather. He took his time reaching the top, and when he did, it was with a combination of disappointment and relief that he discovered she had disappeared.

Patrick, standing alone at the top of the bank, made a decision. He would swim again somehow. He looked out over the difficult whirlpool. He would swim there and take the world above with him, if necessary. This would be his battle and his strength.

This was Friday, the day he had promised to meet the major at the hotel. Patrick would be gathering his own evidence, doing his own research while he listened to the historian's incontestable proof. Learning the woman.

At the edge of the forest he stood for nearly thirty minutes, waiting for the streetcar which would take him up to Main Street. The fog in the air and the slow wind made the whole landscape appear as if it were growing under water.

Later, he could never decide whether the woman had been close enough to see his face.

Approaching the white clapboard of Kick's Hotel, Patrick did not concern himself with thoughts of blood soaking into the soil he walked on. Still, after the lecture, he had discovered that a part of his intellect had become interested in the concept of ownership as it applies to military events. McDougal clearly felt the battle was all his, right down to the last death throes in the dawn hours. The Americans were dismissed, sent back to their own side of the river, giving up, at the moment of retreat, not only their interest in Canada but, if the major had his way, any real participation in the battle. After the lecture, Patrick was able to imagine the American troops, able to visualize them, but always with their backs turned, running away into the morning.

He climbed three wooden steps, crossed the planked verandah, and entered the hotel. Before he could make inquiries he heard McDougal call him from the top of the staircase. The major had obviously been waiting for him, watching his approach from an upper window. In the interior darkness, Patrick could only see the other man as a vague, featureless silhouette. Then he felt the lens in his brain creak open, ready, for the moment, to take in history.

"Let me tell you all about Laura Secord." McDougal broached the subject as he poured the younger man a third cup of tea. "Laura Secord is almost entirely responsible for my career as a military historian."

"What ... did you know her, then?" Patrick began to employ mental arithmetic to determine if this was chronologically possible.

"Only by reputation."

The two men were sitting by the window in McDougal's

rooms. They had an excellent view of the funeral home from there.

"Built right on the Lundy's Lane battlefield, and not much later," McDougal had said, shaking his head at the travesty.

The major's living quarters were not up to much; two rooms filled with books and papers, a few overstuffed chairs, a huge elaborate oak bed and McDougal's desk . . . apparently the site of much activity. Out the window, the undertaker's establishment and Drummond Hill Cemetery rising up behind its roof.

"Laura's buried there, you know," McDougal said, turning in his chair so that he could see the spot. "Not that anyone cares or anything like that. All of this really should be sacred land." The sweep of his arm took in most of Main Street: the greengrocer, the barbershop, the blacksmith near the corner. "Look what the Americans have done with Gettysburg! This country buries its history so fast people with memories are considered insane. The Americans still think they won the 1812 war, which I assure you they did not, and nobody up here gives a damn one way or another."

"About Laura Secord," Patrick nudged the other man gently back to the original subject.

"Ah yes, . . . she came to me in a dream, you see, saying *Remind them, remind them*. I was in college at the time studying anything but Canadian history. I was dreaming a lot too. Don't dream any more for some reason."

"You're joking, of course . . . about her talking to you in the dream."

"No, I certainly am not joking, and under the circumstances, I'd say she had a point. Why *wasn't* I studying Canadian history? Did you know there are no less than three hundred and forty-two books in print in the United States on the subject of the War of 1812?"

No, Patrick didn't know.

"All from their point of view, of course."

"What *is* their point of view?"

"Total victory! They never lost a battle, a skirmish, a cockfight. Arrogant bastards!"

"But some British historians . . ."

"Ah yes, the celebrated British historians. But they were never here, you see." McDougal pointed through the floor, two storeys down to the ground. "According to them, the whole goddam war was fought by gallant sailors, all of British birth, on the briny deep." He threw his hands up in despair. "No credit given to men like Captain Drummond – " he nodded vaguely in the direction of the cemetery – "who was a Canadian by birth. No credit given to Laura Secord. The truth is the Brits dressed some of us up in red uniforms, let some of us fight with pitchforks in our overalls, and then they promptly forgot about all of us. God Save the Fat Unattractive Queen! That's all they care about."

"So, am I to assume that you are going to write a book?"

"Yes, you may assume that. But since no one has given a damn up until now, compiling the information, the papers may take me the rest of my life. I may never finish it . . . never. And now, this summer, I have to have a house built. My wife wants a house."

Patrick's palms began to sweat. Looking around the rooms, he agreed it was no place for a woman. He imagined his own wife's reaction to this setting which screamed of a lack of domesticity. But even so, it would be too confining for the woman in the woods.

"Did you know that she wore a brown cotton dress with little orange flowers printed on it?" McDougal walked across the room and began to straighten some of the papers on his desk. "And she had nothing on her feet but a pair of little leather slippers."

"Your wife?" asked Patrick, eagerly leaning forward in his chair.

"No, no . . . Laura Secord."

Patrick fell back, disappointed but patient. McDougal was looking for something now, something buried beneath the mounds of paper on the desk. "By the time she reached Fitzgibbon's headquarters," the major continued, "the little shoes were lost, her feet were bare. And she had crossed Twelve Mile Creek not once, but twice!" McDougal reached for something situated under a huge pile of documents. "Aha, I've found it!" he announced triumphantly.

In his hand he held a small bronze paperweight fashioned in the shape of a cow. "This," he cried, "is Laura Secord's cow!"

Patrick, thoroughly convinced now that he had lost the thread of conversation, merely stared stupidly at the object in the other man's hand.

"Imagine it," McDougal continued, "the young, slim woman alone, walking through the enemy-infested, beast-ridden woods, and she has the presence of mind to bring a cow along to fool the enemy sentries. Twelve miles over a rough terrain...." McDougal began to walk the bronze cow over the mountains and valleys of his paperwork. "And then ..." he paused and wedged the cow between two portfolios ... "and then she arrives at her destination only to find her path blocked by a company of Indians ... reinforcements, working for our side, but how was she to know? Indians in the moonlight ... awesome! They let her pass, however. They escorted her, in fact to Fitzgibbon, whereupon she gave him the message and we surprised them before they could surprise us. "SURPRISE!!!" he shouted at Patrick, who jumped nervously in his chair.

Silence filled the room as the two men pondered the dead woman's heroic deed. Patrick looked across the cemetery on the hill. "What happened to the cow?" he asked, for want of anything better to say.

"Oh, it's right here," replied McDougal, turning again towards his desk. "I always keep it right here to remind me of Laura ... to remind me of my mission. Remind them, remind them," he quoted from his dream.

Patrick decided to let the matter pass.

McDougal returned to his chair by the window. "May I confess something to you?" he asked with a serious air.

"Of course," replied Patrick.

"My wife is very much like Laura Secord. I think that may be one of the reasons I married her, though God forbid she know that. It's not that she has the pioneering spirit or anything like that, but physically she resembles the Laura that came to me in my dream."

"Remind them, remind them," muttered Patrick. And then, "Where is she now, your wife, I mean?" This last question uttered casually, as if he were merely making polite conversation.

"Now she doesn't even come back here to sleep. I join her in the evenings." McDougal scratched his beard. "She hates it here." He looked around the untidy room. "Can't say as I blame her."

"Where does she go?" Patrick's pulse was beginning to race. "Do you have relatives hereabouts?"

McDougal laughed. "She goes to the woods. We have a piece of property there called Whirlpool Heights. The whirlpool is all ours, you know, the only part of the river that is entirely Canadian. Don't tell the Yankees, though, they'll probably try to conquer it. I've got a tent out there for the summer while the house is being built ... already we've spent a few weeks ... quite pleasant really. You must come out some time. It's a marvellous spot."

"What does she do out there all day?" Patrick asked the question very slowly. He hardly dared to look at the other man while he waited for him to answer.

"She reads books," said McDougal. And then, almost to himself, "She's the closest thing to a compulsive reader I've ever met. Burns them up like fire."

"What kind of books?" asked Patrick, trying to keep the note of urgency out of his voice, but already knowing the answer.

"Now there's a coincidence," said the major. "It's poetry

she mostly reads ... the Brits ... Wordsworth, Coleridge, that sort of stuff. And Browning. She's mad about Browning. She reads far too much Browning, if you ask me. It's unhealthy. Why, I ask, now that I think about it, isn't she reading *you*? Why not something Canadian? Of course, why didn't I think of it, she'll have to meet you. You'll have to meet her." McDougal paused for a moment or two, running the following week's appointments through his mind. "Wednesday evening," he said finally. "You must come Wednesday evening."

Patrick looked uncomfortably at the floor. "I should like that," he said, "very much."

Half an hour later, when he stood to leave, Patrick found that he could look directly into the clothes cupboard on the opposite side of the room. And he was absolutely certain that, hanging there among the more ordinary clothes belonging to the couple, he could see a rather old-fashioned dress of brown cotton. One that had orange flowers printed all over its surface. He quickly took note of the fact that the hem appeared to be ragged and muddy – as if someone had walked in it for a great distance over a wild and rugged terrain.

Once he was outside of the hotel, Patrick looked up at McDougal's window. He had intended to wave but, as the older man was not to be seen, he interrupted the gesture halfway and turned towards the street.

At the funeral home opposite he noticed a small boy standing absolutely still upon the lawn. This was not, Patrick realized as he stared at the child, motion briefly halted. This lack of movement was so complete it conveyed the same disturbing messages as drastic, inexplicable activity.

Patrick himself stood utterly still for some moments watching the boy in amazement. A breeze touched the hair on their heads at exactly the same time. It shook the ribbon

In the evenings of the past, Maud and her husband Charles had agreed never to discuss funerals.

Instead, they discussed spiders.

Not that Maud had particularly wanted to discuss spiders, but when it was a choice between funerals or spiders, what alternative did she have?

"If you wish to grow and thrive," her mother-in-law had always chanted, "let the spiders go alive."

This seemed to Maud to have been a particularly apt piece of advice when applied to her own domestic situation. Charles adored spiders. He admired them. He considered them a superior species and he was determined that they should "Go alive."

The spiders in his collection had been silenced and stilled in the most humane way possible and not, even then, without a generous amount of guilt on the young undertaker's part.

Maud could always tell when Charles had made an addition to his collection. He would be grim and silent for days, cheered only by the fact that he had never allowed the housekeeper to remove a single cobweb from the upper storey of Grady and Son. Downstairs was different. He was not so impractical that he did not understand that, down there, the ceilings should be swept clean. He simply avoided looking up while he was working, as if it had never crossed his mind that a spider might have ever entered the premises.

One night, as Maud sat crocheting in the upstairs parlour underneath a ceiling, which, over the years, had become a complete mesh of aged webs, many of them soiled, broken and deserted, she had decided to broach the subject of house cleaning with her husband, who was reading near the pot-bellied stove. She was intelligent enough to approach the issue from a spider's point of view.

"It would seem unlikely," she had begun, "that we shall have any new spiders in this room. There is just not enough space. Surely a young spider wouldn't want to move in up there . . . among all those wrecks?"

"If they don't like it, let them do something about it," Charles replied. "I'm certainly not going to disturb anything."

Maud was not this easily put off the track. "Perhaps," she continued, "they are simply not strong enough to do anything about it . . . maybe the situation has gotten out of hand and they need help. Then, wouldn't it be a Christian act to remove the webs they don't need . . . the old ones?"

"Spiders *never* need help," Charles had replied, astonished that she had even considered the possibility. "They *always* know exactly what they are doing."

"Supposing the house suddenly filled up with black widows?" Maud was testing. "Surely you'd kill them."

"Black widows have a completely unfair, undeserved reputation. They do *not* bite unless they are threatened, and even then only if they are protecting an egg mass. No, I would *not* kill them. We could live side by side with them quite easily, happily in fact. Anyway, there aren't any around here. Or, at least, not very many."

Charles had managed to find one though, in an abandoned out-house and, because they were so rare, he was forced to add it to his collection. A particularly depressing day.

He had recounted in detail how the spider had made no effort to escape when he had trapped it in a little box and how, later, it had accepted the chloroform as if it had always known its fate. (Like an Irish patriot going to the gallows, his mother had sighed, sentimentally.) A particularly brave and dignified spider for whom Charles had felt nothing but affection and respect.

Maud secretly admired the black widow. She knew that the female ate the male after mating which seemed only fair since there existed male spiders who actually wrapped females up and tied them down before impregnating them. A shocking variety of insect rape!

"Which spider is it that wraps up his mate?" she asked her husband.

"The thrice-banded crab spider."

"Why does he do that to her?"

"Why not?"

Maud let it go. She had learned early on that she should never criticize a spider, but even more important, she should never touch one. One of their most loquacious marital quarrels had concerned the removal of a daddy-long-legs from their bedroom. Charles had told her repeatedly the daddy-long-legs was not a spider; that spiders had waists and daddy-long-legs did not. It took her no time at all, therefore, to dispose of one once it had foolishly entered their bedchamber. What she didn't know was that Charles had spotted it there earlier in the day.

Before climbing into bed that night he had begun to search the floors and windows.

"Where is the daddy-long-legs?"

"It wasn't a spider."

"What did you do with it?"

"It didn't have a waist." And then, when the tension seemed unbearable, "It wouldn't have made a web."

"What did you do with him?"

Maud had looked heavenward, up to a ceiling like gauze. "What could it possibly matter? Besides, they bite."

Charles had turned white with fury. "Where did you put him!?" he had shouted, moving ominously closer.

"They mate without courtship," she had thrown out hopefully, showing off how much she had learned, even in the few short years of their marriage.

He had turned to look directly at her and in a calm, terrifying voice, he had said, "You killed him. I can't believe it, you actually killed him."

"Yes," she confessed.

"Murderer!" he yelled.

Cornered, she turned on him. "You were the one . . . you told me they weren't spiders. I can't be expected to preserve every insect in the world. I demand the right to kill every bug I want to." Prudent even in anger, she added, "Everything except spiders."

"Spiders are *not* bugs! Neither was the daddy-long-legs, and you killed him!" He looked at her with hatred. "You wanted to kill him. You *enjoyed* killing him." And then, after a long furious silence, "Find him!"

"Charles, he's squashed, you wouldn't want to . . ."

"FIND HIM!!"

Weeping, Maud had spent an hour picking through the trash in the kitchen looking for the crumpled body of the daddy-long-legs. She sorted through coffee grounds, orange peels, mouldy peas, broken crockery, and soggy newspapers. When, at last, she appeared in the bedroom doorway with the small bundle in her outstretched hand, Charles had simply waved it aside with a gesture of despair so complete Maud's anger almost turned to compassion.

She occasionally surprised herself by becoming immersed in memories like this. In some she played an active role, in others her function was passive. These private dramas acted themselves out in her inner theatre just when she was certain she had forgotten Charles altogether. Then an anecdote he had told her would, inexplicably, assert itself in her mind; the stories he had recounted about events that took place when she was not present becoming, for the moment, stronger than her own personal past, more intensely visual, until, at times, she thought of herself as the keeper of his memories rather than the keeper of his memory.

Today, she was once again at her desk in the sunroom, notebook open on the oak wood, a scrap of paper to the left of it containing the information she should have been recording. She had slipped away, however, from the activity and the pen lay discarded in the spine of the book. Her arms were crossed and her head hung slightly downwards. She was having a memory of one of Charles' memories.

He had been walking in the Niagara Glen on a spring morning, quite early, examining the webs of shamrock spiders while they were still covered with dew, shining in the sun. A completely safe activity since he had captured both a male and a female shamrock spider years ago when he had first begun to collect. They were very common and in this memory Maud could see hundreds of their glimmering webs decorating the edges of the patch on which Charles walked. She could see Charles, too, bending down, now and then, to study them more closely.

He had told her that this particular kind of spider ate its daily web. Maud had responded to this with "Give us this day our daily web." Charles had liked that. Then he told her that each night the spider constructed a new web, in complete darkness, by touch alone. This was one of the things about spiders that truly astonished Maud ... the idea of them there in the pitch black, their delicate legs working on webs while the rest of the world slept on. She thought that was remarkable.

There had been trilliums everywhere that morning, thousands of them if she were to believe Charles, and although he was not much interested in flowers, unless they guaranteed special spiders, even he had been amazed by their variety, particularly by the odd, normally white, flower with a splash of red at its heart. Painted trilliums, she had told him; quite rare.

Satisfied that all was well in the world of the shamrock spider, Charles had been about to turn back when he saw someone approaching him on the path; a tall man with a moustache, one who wore military boots and carried a walking stick.

The two men had begun a conversation about the glories of the morning and the beauty of nature in general until Charles had heard a strange rattling sound coming from the man's stick.

He had hardly believed his eyes. Tied to the other man's walking stick was an enormous rattlesnake. Maud, immersed in the memory, could see the man, the stick, the snake. She could hear the frightening noise. The man had prudently tied the head of the rattler to the bottom of the stick, away from his hands. A leather thong kept the head firmly in place while the body wound around and around the stick. The snake couldn't strike even had it wanted to.

Charles had been so shocked, so horrified that he had not thought to ask the man what he intended to do with the snake. Maud could see the way Charles' hands had moved as he described the incident to her, making a spiral in the air to show how the snake's body surrounded the stick, then making a fist near the floor to represent the snake's fearsome head. He had estimated that the creature must have been at least four feet long.

Maud came, now, slowly, slowly back; back from the Niagara Glen and the morning filled with silver webs spun in darkness, back from the terror of the snake, and then back from the parlour four years ago where Charles told his story. Maud never knew, would never know now, who the other man was.

She sat quickly upright in her chair as she became conscious of being away in the memory of her dead husband's memories. Shaking the images from in front of her eyes, out of her mind, she returned to the task before her and wrote:

> *Body of a Man Found at Maid of the Mist Landing*
>   *July 3rd, 1889*

then, after pausing to refill her pen, she continued:

> *Dark grey hair*
> *Narrow leather belt*
> *Laundry mark D.N.*
> *Heavy fleece-lined underdrawers*
> *Corduroy pants*
> *Shoe about number 9, plain without toe caps*
> *Fleece-lined undershirt with marker (D.N.)*
> *Blue polka dot handkerchief*
> *Half a packet of Fashion smoking tobacco*
> *Bone pipe stem with silver funnel*
> *Also a Peterson pipe*
> *25 cents Canadian and 10 cents American*
> *Good teeth*
> *About 5 ft. 10 inches in height*

Who was this man, this D.N.? She would more than likely never know. Who was the keeper of his memories?

There was something tragic, not about his battered body, necessarily, but about his blue polka dot handkerchief, his Fashion smoking tobacco, his Peterson pipe.

Earlier in the morning she had taken all these sad relics into the long hall cupboard where she kept the possessions of the nameless floaters. There, as she had so many times before, she placed the objects in a numbered canvas sack and left them on a shelf with all the others. As there were no windows in the cupboard she had brought along a lamp and in its light the sacks crouched on the shelves like a herd of small docile animals, each shaped slightly differently from the next, but all undeniably of the same species.

This cupboard was Maud's own personal reliquary. She wanted to enclose and protect the fragmented evidence of these smothered lives, to hold memories of their memories.

This was her museum.

All these spider conversations from the past had been running through her mind just when she least expected them. Maud looked at the doily that decorated the arm of the chair across the room. There it rested looking for all the world like a well-ordered web; round, white, transparent. Something a marbled-orb-web-weaver might have made but wouldn't, Maud knew, because it was utterly useless.

Before she left the desk she remembered two things: that the night of the daddy-long-legs quarrel she had dreamt about spiders, egg sacs, and webs, and that nine months later the child had been born.

*

Patrick waited until it was almost dark before he set out to visit the major and his wife at Whirlpool Heights. It had been a long time since he had dined in broad daylight, and then he had hardly eaten, barely understood the conversation which passed between his uncle and aunt.

He had spent the afternoon in his room, frightened by his obsession concerning the woman in the woods. He could say nothing about her. There were no poems connected to her. This was not a lyrical experience. It was a fixed state of mind.

He realized that in his imagination, his fantasy, she was completely still. The woods moved around her like part of her nervous system or electrical impulses suddenly becoming visible outside her brain. Even though he had seen her walk (shoulders in a straight line) towards and then away from him, the idea of any activity taken as a decision on her part did not connect with his vision of her. The first image. She, reading, slowly turning the pages, not moving as the forest moved around her. The first image. He held to that. Blue dress, white hand on the book's cover, more trilliums than he had ever seen before opening all around her.

As he climbed the cedar fence at the end of his uncle's orchard, the last light of day was fading from the sky. A late trolley, filled with tourists, moved slowly down the edge of River Road. Many of the women held huge bouquets of wildflowers they had picked earlier in the afternoon. Some of the blossoms were already dead and drooped sadly over the women's arms, others had merely closed up for the night. The windows of the vehicle were open and through them Patrick could hear not the slightest sound of conversation. Tired picnickers drifting back to town.

Now that he had become accustomed to the act of hiding, the act of watching, walking openly through the woods at this time filled him with anxiety. He felt instinctively for the fieldglasses, instruments of distance. He started at the sound of his own footsteps, of small branches brushing his sleeve. As Patrick approached the spot, he saw, to his surprise, two different lights through the trees. One bright and moving, easily recognizable as the campfire; the other a strange, still, glowing shape, not as readily identifiable. It wasn't until he was almost there that he knew he had been looking at the tent, illuminated from within by coal-oil lamps. And by then he was close enough to see the woman's shadow, clearly silhouetted against the tent wall.

He could also see McDougal pacing up and down in front of the fire awaiting his guest's arrival. The major shouted something in the direction of the tent. The shadow inside began to change, to move towards the entrance. Patrick heard a strong female voice responding to McDougal's and he immediately stopped walking.

He didn't want her to have a voice, did not wish to face the actuality of her speech, how words would change the shape of her mouth, stiffen the relaxed bend of her neck which he had seen when he watched her read. One more step on his part and she would leave, forever, the territory of his dream and he would lose something – some power, some privacy, some control.

McDougal turned his head towards the path as though listening to a sound he couldn't quite interpret. Patrick slipped behind a fir tree. He heard the woman call her husband

and, abruptly, Patrick turned his back to the lights he had been looking at, and began to move away.

The walk back to the farm was difficult; moonless, dark and silent. Several times Patrick lost the path and found himself immersed in a web of tangled, invisible branches. Once, only once, he got himself totally turned around, losing his sense of direction so completely he was astonished to see the glow of the tent, once again, in the distance. All the while, as he stumbled blindly along, he attempted to disconnect the shadow he had seen, the voice he had heard, from the woman he'd been watching in the woods.

A few days later Patrick allowed McDougal to take him down to the whirlpool. He had stopped by the hotel to apologize for his failure to appear on the appointed evening. His uncle, he said, had wanted him at the farm. Something to do with a sick cow.

"Laura's cow," McDougal replied, "must have been unusually healthy to walk all that way in rough conditions."

Patrick asked about the whirlpool. How far was it from the acre? Would they be able to see it from the house?

McDougal responded with enthusiasm. "We'll go!" he announced. "We'll go right now." He consulted his watch. "Trolley in seven minutes. I'll show you."

"But your wife," said Patrick, on the verge of declining the invitation, "she won't be expecting us."

"She's not there," replied the major, as he searched for his walking stick. "Even *she* has to occasionally go into town. You know ... provisions. This is her afternoon to shop in Queenston."

Shop. The word sounded mundane, factual, almost impossible in terms of the woman as Patrick wanted her.

And so, after a brief perusal of the acre he was already so familiar with, Patrick allowed himself to be taken down to the whirlpool by McDougal, behaving – so that the major would describe it, talk about it – as if he had never seen it before.

McDougal was delighted to be showing someone the property, the water, and the scenery. He ran back and forth, pointing out geological formations and strange plants, almost as if he had created the landscape himself.

It wasn't until they reached the surprisingly gentle ribbon of beach at the edge of the whirlpool that Patrick began to speak. "It's really rather like a dream, isn't it? I mean all this wild landscape and then the American factories just around the bend where you can't see them."

"I don't dream," McDougal answered, staring through the transparent water to the shallow bed near the shore, "but my wife does. Dreams a lot about water. Damndest dreams, she has."

"What dreams?" Patrick wanted him to continue.

"They could be nightmares, but she says they're not. She's always falling, or flying down from a great height towards a river at the bottom. Then as she gets nearer and nearer the river ... nearer the point of impact ... yes, I'm sure she says she's falling. Oh look." McDougal bent down to pick a small white flower. "Do you know this species?"

"She is falling ..." Patrick wanted to bring him back to the woman's dream.

"Yes, she must be falling because it always ends with her crashing. Death, I suppose. If she had been flying, like a bird, she would have merely settled down. Right?"

"What else does she say?" asked Patrick quickly, astonished at the direction the conversation was taking; that the dream woman was being revealed as a dreamer herself.

"Oh, she rants on and on about what a wonderful image it makes ... something about each stone, each pebble, so clear ... the water making everything underneath so precise ... rushing up towards her. Sounds like a nightmare to me."

"It would probably be a burst of colour," Patrick mused, "those pebbles, like fireworks, but not at all the colour of – "

"Don't talk to me about fireworks," McDougal interjected at this point. "I'm tired of the Yankees and their fireworks."

"And then ... ?" Patrick wanted to draw the major back to the subject of the woman, her dream.

"Then they get ridiculously patriotic, wave their silly flags, shoot off cannons, claim to have won the War of 1812."

"Was it the whirlpool she was dreaming about?"

"Who?" asked McDougal. "Oh, Fleda. She didn't say. She thinks I made up that Laura Secord dream of mine, by the way. It's the only dream I ever had and she thinks I invented it." He scowled at the water. "And she's never had one single authentically Canadian dream. Even if she did dream about Laura she'd never admit it to me." McDougal looked across the wide whirlpool. "All this water," he said vaguely.

"I mean," said Patrick, trying not to show his impatience, "does she dream about the whirlpool now?" Attempting to appear casual, he gently kicked, with one boot, at a small pile of stones wedged in the corner of a bent, sunken branch.

"I can't remember. Last week she dreamt something about the house, I think." McDougal was still looking at the water. "I wonder what General Brock's dreams were like. Perhaps they were filled with musket fire." He turned to Patrick. "Do poets dream? I mean at night?"

"As little as possible," Patrick replied hastily, wanting more about the woman. "What was her house dream like?"

"Let me see. . . . Oh yes, she dreamed the house was the whirlpool . . . no, I'm wrong, she said the whirlpool lived in the house . . . though she couldn't see it. As long as she was in the house she was always being pushed around by it in a circular fashion from room to room to room. But it wasn't like water, she said, more like a strong current of air." The major laughed. "Really, it's totally foolish. If I'd had a dream like that I would have forgotten it instantly."

Patrick, who had taken the flower from McDougal earlier, now moved it nervously from hand to hand.

McDougal picked up a stone and threw it as far as he

could out into the water, as if he were trying to send a signal to the centre of the whirlpool.

"How did she feel about that house?" Patrick eventually asked.

The major laughed again. "How would she know? She was too busy being moved from room to room." He turned his back to the water. "What strange dreams she has. Too much Browning, I expect."

"I am going to swim this whirlpool," Patrick announced, and for just a moment he pictured himself gliding through the woman's dream.

The major stared at him, speechless.

"I haven't quite decided whether I will go around it with the current or if I will head straight across from one side to the other." Had the whirlpool, he wondered, suddenly become architecture or flesh? Would he be able to tour it like a museum or caress it as he would a woman?

"Now listen – " McDougal pointed up the river – "Captain Webb tried to swim those rapids just a couple of years ago. You know, the *famous* Captain Webb. He ended up as dead as a doornail. Stick to poetry, my boy, that's my advice."

Patrick ignored his warning. "I have no intention of swimming the rapids, just the whirlpool."

"*Just* the whirlpool," snorted McDougal. "Impossible . . . can't be done."

"I used to be a marvellous swimmer," Patrick said, almost to himself. And then, turning to the major: "Tell me some of the things you've observed about the whirlpool, it might help me." Suddenly, he was uncertain whether it was the water or the woman he was talking about.

"Nothing will help you," McDougal said bluntly. "It simply can't be done."

Both men were silent for some time. Patrick noticed a fish leap up from the current then disappear again beneath the surface. Shining and uninjured by contact with the dangerous whirlpool it had looked like a coin being tossed in the sun.

"May I see that flower?" demanded McDougal, wishing to turn the conversation from a topic he was not taking very seriously. He studied the plant for a moment. "Rattlesnake plantain," he said. "Or, if you prefer the Latin, *Goodyera repens*." He handed the blossom back to Patrick.

"And your wife," asked Patrick, "does she know anything about the whirlpool – besides what she sees in her dreams?"

"No," replied the major, "she doesn't know a thing about it really, nothing about geology. There used to be another river here, you see." He pointed towards the ravine through which they had descended to reach the spot on which they now stood. "Then the ice age came along and filled it up with rocks and soil."

"So there used to be a fork in the river here, then, am I right? And now some of the water still wants to go that route. But, of course, it can't because there is nowhere to go so it turns back on itself."

"Right. But when I explain that to my wife she perceives it as a metaphor or some such thing. Talks about interrupted journeys. As if the river were Ulysses or something."

That's it exactly, thought Patrick, amazed, delighted. He smiled at McDougal with genuine warmth, knowing that this man would answer his questions, tell him everything he wanted to hear.

Patrick's idea of the woman was beginning to solidify. She was a dreamer, living in the open, perceiving whirlpools as metaphors. How easy the landscape seemed to be for her. Awake, she watched it and lived inside it. Asleep she dreamed it. Perhaps the woman *was* the landscape. Patrick was attracted to this idea of her. He wanted to become a part of the impression.

Ø

103

10 July 1889

Rain today. David out at the camp. Imagine him there encouraging the men to ride horses on the slippery ground. Orders.

Last night he told me that his friend, the poet, had been asking about my dreams. How strange . . . though David doesn't seem to think so. Certainly no poet has been interested in my dreams before. David says that it has something to do with the whirlpool, that he wants to swim it. They talked about my water dream. When I asked David what this man looked like he merely replied, "Young."

How young? How tall? What colour of eyes? I wanted to know. David said he would bring a collection of this man's verses back from the hotel.

I stood for some time at the edge of the bank this morning and looked down at the whirlpool, trying to imagine how a poet would swim it and why he would want to. Two small, dark figures were pulling something out of the water but I was too far away to see what it was. Perhaps one of them was the Old River Man . . . tidying up his river.

This afternoon I have stayed inside the tent reading Browning and, for some reason, thinking about the house David and I abandoned nearly two years ago.

What I remember most about leaving it was emptying the cupboards.

Such debris! Such endless rooms filled with kept things! Such hoarding behind such firmly closed doors. Everything out of sight for years. Shoes, belts, corsets, stockings, gloves, buckles, feathers, shawls, hats, hat-boxes.

Plates, cups, saucers, vases, urns, relish dishes, mustard pots, salt and pepper shakers, candle snuffers, silver trays, pickle tongs, cruets, spooners, goblets, sealer jars.

And behind the doors of the upright cupboard in the parlour: papers, papers, old letters, newspaper clippings, recipes, photographs of deceased uncles, and of distant cousins, a survey of the property.

What is marriage, then, if not an accumulation of objects?

And if I were to leave the tent that I live in now, what would I take with me? Something to sleep on and underneath, matches for a fire. The stars, the moon, the sun. A memory of the whirlpool, a memory of Browning. . . .

Last night when I began to talk I spoke about industry ruining landscape, about factories and mines. About cities and living in them. About railway terminals and shipping offices. David talked about the war. We didn't, somehow, seem to be speaking to each other.

Soon we both became very quiet.

There were no stars, no moon outside. I went to the rain barrel to get water to extinguish the remains of the fire. Steam and smoke in yellow light.

Later I took the lantern to the edge of the bank and sent a path of light, first down the bank to the whirlpool, then back through the forest towards the road.

> "O how dark your villa was
> Windows fast and obdurate
> How the garden grudged me grass
> Where I stood – the iron gate
> Ground its teeth to let me past"
> R.B.   A Serenade at the Villa

Obdurate: Hardened in evil; insensible to moral influence,
unyielding, relentless, hard-hearted, inexorable.
  Nobody's angel.

I

Now Patrick understood that, like a child at play, observed, but not conscious of observation, the woman would reveal sides of herself to him that she had revealed to no one else. He would experience her when she was whole, not fragmented into considerations of self and other. Part of this process would involve his already skilful hidden observations, his ability to camouflage himself in forests, his cunning conversations with her husband, his almost magical talent for abrupt departures.

But he needed more. He wanted her past as well; her recent history, the seasons she had lived through before the tent, the architecture she had abandoned. It seemed to him that what she had left behind might be as significant as what she had subsequently chosen. He wanted an utter comprehension of the forces that had moved her into the forest, what she had seen and listened to on winter mornings, which chair she most often occupied, her favourite window. He wanted to know how she had managed her apparently fearless letting go – of domestic architecture, of closed spaces – how she had been able to turn away in order to embrace the open. He wanted to discover the exact moment when the whirlpool had taken hold of her life.

In the mornings, when he crouched in the woods watching her read, tend flowers, wash china, keep the fire, he saw the woman as she was now. When her chores were completed, he visited the whirlpool with her, watched her launch tiny boats, listened to her singing, memorized the tunes.

In the afternoons, he visited the world she had left behind. He boarded the streetcar and rode it into town, certain that his arrival would follow McDougal's departure for the camp, avoiding Fridays when the major worked in his rooms all day. He strolled casually up and down the wooden sidewalk that bordered the street outside the hotel, attempting to reconstruct *her* walking there, picturing her boots on the planks when they were covered with snow, or darkened by rain, or blanketed with maple leaves. He thought about the rocking chairs on the verandah. Had she ever sat in them? Did her mind slip down to the whirlpool as the furniture rocked under her weight? Had she read there? Who, if anyone, had she spoken to?

Mostly, however, his attempts to find even a trace of her there were unsuccessful. She was chained, in his mind, to the whirlpool, to the woods. To the tent and to the fire. But certainly he believed that his repeated exposure to this abandoned geography *must* result in some form of understanding about the lure of the whirlpool, its organic pull. What he was trying to discover was what had made her select that part of the forest, which he had merely stumbled across by chance.

Today, he decided he would examine the opposite side of the street, the places which, in the course of the ordinary events which made up the other seasons of her life, she must have visited on shopping errands. The grocer's, the butcher's, the post office. He mailed a postcard of the waterfall to his wife, saying that he missed her, lying. He could not, for the life of him, imagine the woman in the forest buying stamps. Who would she be writing to, about what? Still he went through the motions, attempting to become her in the act of pushing mail across the counter.

Back on the sidewalk once again he stood directly across

from the hotel and looked up to the windows which he knew were McDougal's, knowing she would never have done this but curious nonetheless. A tree grew directly in front of one of the windows but the views from the other three were unobstructed. Now he was part of that view, a thin young man in dark clothes leaning against a white picket fence, looking into a spot that she at one time must have looked out of. But what could he learn from this? Nothing more than the fact that he was on the wrong side. He tried to remember something about the windows from his visit with the major. Had the sills been painted, were they dusty, was the glass clean? He recalled the view, the landscape he was now briefly part of, but nothing of the opposite side of the windows – could not even say with certainty whether or not there were curtains. Perhaps these details were unimportant. It was the woman's enclosure there and her looking out that mattered.

As he stood there, looking up, his mind filled with glass and leaves as he believed hers must have been at one time or another, a word caught him unawares. Barely a whisper, it fluttered somewhere near the back part of his brain so that he thought that what he was listening to was wind in the trees, or even the small noises his starched shirt made against his jacket when he shifted position. The word was "Nothing."

Patrick was not, at first, distracted by it, attributing it to air currents. He wanted to picture how raindrops on the opposite side of the glass might appear to a woman looking out and was concentrating upon that. But when he caught it a second and then a third time, he was forced to turn and seek its source which, he was surprised to discover, was the mouth of the small boy he had seen standing in this yard before. "Nothing," the boy was saying, pointing to the window which had until now held Patrick's attention.

"Nothing?" Patrick asked, confused.

"Nothing," the boy replied conclusively.

Patrick stared at the child who stood directly behind the picket fence which surrounded the undertaking establishment. He was dressed in a marine-blue waistcoat and knee britches and had a small, worn, featureless toy tucked under one elbow. He might have been any age between three and six.

"Nothing," he said again, still not looking at the man he apparently addressed.

"What's nothing?" asked Patrick.

"Noth-ing," said the child, carefully enunciating both syllables.

"Yes, but where?"

"Be-reavement," said the child.

"Whose bereavement?" asked Patrick, surprised.

"Sorrow," replied the child with a bored sigh, something close to a yawn. "Wheelbarrow."

"Have you lost your wheelbarrow?"

The child stroked his toy and looked absently around the yard. "Floater," he said vaguely.

Patrick attempted to recall how one was supposed to behave in the presence of small children. Lollipops and storybooks sprang into his mind along with other, more improvisational possibilities – string games and shadowy animals made upon walls by wringing your hands in the path of a coal-oil lamp. He did not, however, have the former objects on his person and he had never mastered the skills of the latter performances.

"What's your name?" he asked the child.

"Parlour," said the boy, moving his free arm back and forth across the flower garden immediately in front of him. "Aug-ust," he continued.

"No," said Patrick, "July now, August next."

The child gazed down the street at an approaching trolley. "Sofa," he announced and nodded wisely.

Intrigued, Patrick searched his pockets for something to give to the boy. He finally decided upon a nickel, which he placed in the flat centre of his palm as he reached over the fence.

"Onion," said the boy.

"Nickel," said Patrick.

The child was not to be moved. He retaliated with the word "shovel."

"No," said Patrick patiently, "nickel ... this is a nickel ... for you."

The child stroked his toy and ignored the coin. "Salad fork!" he sang as the trolley, making a great deal of noise, rolled by. "Ri-ver."

Patrick looked back towards the windows of the hotel. He wondered what it would be like to be a man on the inside, watching a woman walk over to the window, pause, draw the curtain aside, and look down into the street. For a single instant he saw her figure, darkly dressed and surrounded by the light that moved in from the outside, through glass, to the room. And in that instant he knew everything that would have been in her mind. She would not merely be a woman looking out, she would be a woman wanting out.

"River!" The child's word rang in Patrick's daydream like an awakening angelus, forcing him out of the cool dark of the imagined room, back onto the street. He glanced at the trolley as it moved into the distance and said the word "streetcar," slowly and distinctly, turning, as he enunciated it, back towards the boy.

"Ri-ver," the child said again, stubbornly but without his original exuberance, and then, pointing to the fence, "blossom."

This child, these words, disconnected from their sources, began to astound Patrick, to set up ridiculous yet poetic associations. All at once he was certain that, when he visited the river in the future, he would be unable to do so without conjuring streetcars in his imagination. Likewise, from this day on, he supposed that journeys on streetcars would include water moving behind his forehead. Finally, this idea delighted him. The child's uttered nonsense was a revelation, not unlike the intoxicating leaps he had known himself to take, only once or twice, in the manipulation of language. Suddenly Patrick wanted to experiment with the child, to lay his own obsessions out in front of him like clothes on a bed, just to experience the words this boy might attach to them. He wanted to expose all. Suddenly, by virtue of its very randomness, the child's speech became profound.

"Woman," Patrick began, tentatively, almost with embarrassment.

"Thunder," the child replied immediately.

"Forest," said Patrick.

"Cellar door." The boy pointed up to the sky.

"Swimming." Patrick held his breath, waiting for a response.

"Keeping," said the boy, and then, as if sensing the importance of the subject, he added the word "collar."

"Whirlpool," Patrick ventured, looking directly, and with emotion, into the little face.

"Oh," said the boy, reaching with his free arm across the barrier, the fence, catching Patrick's cuff in his small hand. "Oh, oh, oh," he sighed, rubbing his chest against the fabric that he found there. Then he looked up at the man who had been talking to him and repeated every word they had spoken, quite tenderly and carefully.

⃰

Inside Grady and Son, Maud Grady climbed the stairs holding the child's fist firmly in her hand.

"Thunder woman," he whispered.

"What do you mean by that?" she asked quickly and with the slight twitch that visited the left side of her face when she was annoyed. "What on earth. . . ." She checked herself and, after searching the boy's face for a moment, she laughed, remembering that he would have no idea what he was saying.

She had just finished giving instructions to the men downstairs where they had been preparing for the summer's inevitable stuntman.

They were working mostly in secret, for preparation in an undertaking establishment was not something the community approved of, even in circumstances such as these. In fact, when sixty years before, the first Drummondville Grady had decided to stockpile coffins before they were ordered, no one spoke to him on the street for a fortnight. This was considered, among other things, to be both highly immoral and bad luck. In the outlying concessions it was rumoured that you could predict the number of infant deaths over the winter by counting the number of coffins in Jim Grady's stable, as if he were the grim reaper himself. Years later, when he had purchased a second hearse, the Methodist minister of the time had preached a pointed sermon which he titled "The Wages of Death."

It would not be proper for Maud to be present at the time of the performance. "Looking for business," the town matrons would whisper as they had the first, and last time she attempted to visit an ailing friend. Maud had been shaken then, deeply hurt, knowing that business would come to her whether she looked for it or not. Now she knew which clubs to avoid, which social events to stay away from. The Historical Society, dedicated to facts and personalities already buried, was almost safe. But even there she made it a habit never to be seen in the company of someone whose relative might have taken a turn for the worse.

In the back room, on the ground floor, the three men who worked for Maud scrubbed up their equipment like housewives expecting an important guest. Laying down their money beside the sink, they bet on the outcome. Jas the carpenter, almost reluctantly, in favour of success; Sam the embalmer, and the second carpenter Peter, for failure.

Sam was speaking now. "The last one was a mess. The River Man was fishing him out for days!" He scratched his balding head. "What's a man supposed to do with something like that? Certainly couldn't have recommended an open coffin."

"A couple *have* made it," Jas interjected.

"Yes, but the damned fools feel they have to do it again." He patted a nearby coffin. "Sooner or later they all end up right here."

"Pretty in the cradle, ugly on the table," Peter mumbled.

The other two men laughed.

On the wall beside the window a calendar, topped by a chromo litho of the Falls, announced the month of April. The embalmer walked across the room and tore off three successive sheets of paper.

"It's a form of suicide, I suppose," he said, crumpling

April in his slim hands. "But at least we know it's happening. I like these fellas a damn sight better than the ones who spend the winter locked in the ice – " he disposed of the month of May – "or the ones who don't surface for a month or two . . . God!" He threw June into the garbage in disgust.

The other two men were silent. All of them knew about the ugliness of floaters.

"Lord," he went on, "give me train wrecks, carriage accidents, murder victims, disasters of war, but spare me from floaters!"

The smell, the men knew, lingered for days.

"Now take your tightrope walkers," Peter began, changing the subject. "Your average tightrope walker hereabouts is just not the suicidal type. He could be walking that rope in a tent or over the Grand Canyon . . . chances are just the same that he'll make it to the other side and he *knows* it. But these fellas in their rapid-shooting contraptions, what in Sam Hill do they think is going to happen to them?"

The embalmer was looking far off into space. "Remember that Italian girl, the one who went across with buckets on her feet and a skirt way up to here?" He gestured to his thighs, vaguely at crotch level.

The image of that lady's pink thighs appeared simultaneously in all three men's imaginations.

"Wasn't she something?" Sam continued dreamily. "I'd like to have her next to the wall on a Saturday night . . . buckets and all!"

Now she appeared to them once again, this time flat on her back with her buckets sticking straight up in the air.

"They say Blondin took a stove out there and fried an egg," said Jas, who liked a fantasy as much as any man but believed, as a result of a strict upbringing, that you should never discuss such things.

But the embalmer wasn't listening. "Some said she wore pink stockings but I could swear those thighs were as bare as God made them." He walked over to the window. "And her arms too ... you know, that girl hardly had any clothes on at all."

All up and down Main Street, as far as Sam could see from the window, families were beginning their trek down the hill towards the river. Some were clustered around the place where the streetcar stopped; others had obviously decided to go it on foot. All carried provisions: picnic baskets, blankets, umbrellas, folding chairs, fieldglasses, spy glasses, handkerchiefs (in case of an overwhelmingly moving disaster), megaphones (to cheer on or curse at the stunt man), babies wrapped in tight bundles with bonnets twice the size of their tiny bodies. It was a restless crowd whose emotions were torn between a feigned concern for the safety of the daredevil and a more honest desire for blood. All those over the age of five were discussing the outcome of similar exploits, savouring the goriest details while shaking their heads at the impetuosity of the human spirit.

Today, a young man named Buck O'Connor, who came from no farther away than Grimsby, was to shoot the whirlpool rapids in a vehicle he had constructed himself from the antlers and the tanned hides of several moose he had killed on hunting trips over the years. "Durned fool!" Sam had said. "He won't look nearly as good as a dead moose when he's finished."

The young man claimed, however, that the tanned hide of a moose is stronger than steel, and less dangerous since it gives, rather than breaks, under pressure. Moreover, he contended, moose antlers were known to be almost entirely unbreakable. His contraption, labelled "The Mighty Moose," had been on display for a week now, at a quarter a peek, down at the Maid of the Mist Landing. Even the children who went down there to look at it came away believing Buck hadn't a prayer.

"Goddam!" Peter the carpenter had said, returning to

Grady and Son after viewing the rig. "That thing'll be torn to pieces faster than you can say knife."

"Guess I'd better thread my needle," sighed Sam the embalmer.

The three men locked the workshop door and let themselves out by the back. They walked across the garden to the stables, Jas pointing out the pansies as they passed.

"Larger than usual, I'd say."

The two horses, whom Sam had named Jesus Christ and God Almighty, were bridled, ready to go, hitched up to a wagon with a seat in the front which could accommodate all three men. They walked past it and climbed the open wooden stairs to the stable's attic.

"The question is," said Sam, pushing back the straw hat he always wore on special occasions, "will it be wicker or tin?"

"Wicker," said Peter, moving towards the coffin-shaped basket. "If he doesn't make it he won't be in the river long enough to smell."

ℐ

I "Now you'll see," said David McDougal to his wife as he made preparations to leave the vicinity of the tent. "Now you'll see what the river can do."

"It's total nonsense," she replied, "these men flinging themselves into the rapids, as if the river cared. Why do you always think you have to conquer something just because it's there. *I* already *know* what the river can do. No one has to prove it to me."

"Don't you think it's rather mythical," David continued, "the dangerous quest-like journey, braving the elements in the body of an animal. You should like that. A good image, don't you think? And that poet will be there. Maybe he will write a poem about it."

He entered the tent and returned a few minutes later with an umbrella. Fleda added a few more branches to the fire.

"What an odd fellow that poet is," said McDougal. "That business about swimming – if I know poets, he'll probably just write a poem about it."

"Does he say he wants to write about it?" asked Fleda, imagining a metaphysical response to the whirlpool.

"Did you know," David asked, ignoring her question, "that the Yankees, in retreat from the Lundy's Lane fiasco, actually tried to swim the river? Or at least some of them. They *were* in retreat, by the way. Don't let anyone try to tell you otherwise."

"What are his poems like?" asked Fleda. "Did you bring some for me to read?"

"You're not actually becoming interested in Canadian Letters?" asked David, "Well it's about time. His poems are . . . well . . . short."

"Short? That's all you have to say?"

"Yes, short . . . and with lots of pine trees."

"Then, I'm not interested."

"How can you not be interested? All you ever think about is poetry."

"I am interested in the English poets."

"Why? Because of the pine trees? Look around you – " David gestured to the left and right – "you can't live in this country and ignore pine trees."

"No English poet," said Fleda, "would spend a lot of time worrying about pine trees."

"But," thundered McDougal, becoming quite angry, "*this* is not England!"

After her husband marched testily away Fleda looked at the dark pines that surrounded her and knew that her argument had been with David, not with the poet's choice of subject matter. She had secretly, all the while, been imagining poems filled with the smell of cedars carried on the breath of a northern wind. Scotch pines, white pines. Roots in the ground, needles in the sky.

She walked to the part of bank where she could see the beach through the foliage. From that height the crowd looked to her like a large dark stain growing at the edge of the whirlpool. Wondering how Wordsworth or Browning would interpret landscape such as this or events such as these, she turned away.

She absolutely refused to take part in it. She felt alien, completely different, distant. She could not understand why her husband would want to be a witness, to watch a man who killed animals kill himself inside an animal. At moments like these the separation that she felt from the world expanded to include a separation from her husband. He had become worldly and she had noticed, as he walked away, his awkwardness, his lack of grace. He talked and talked, always in the way men did, moving his arms in jerky, ridiculous ways, wishing to express his point physically. Fleda was bored by him, at this moment, by the physical fact of him. She wished he would simply stop . . . stop walking, stop talking, making his foolish points.

Inside the tent she spread the plaid blanket on the floor and leaned her back against the edge of the bed. All through the next hour, through the cheers and the later groans of the crowd down at the river, she did not look up. She was reading Browning's "In a Balcony."

baa, black sheep, Patrick crooned inside his head. *Yes sir, yes sir*, he sang, keeping his eyes directly between the two bowler hats in front of him through which he could see the water. *Little Bo Peep*, he began silently. Then he felt the straining belly of the man behind him brush his back, and a sudden nausea began to creep upwards from his knees.

Further down the bank a man with a megaphone was making an announcement: LADIES AND GENTLEMEN, YOU ARE HERE TO WITNESS A FEAT OF AMAZING VALOUR, A DEATH-DEFYING SPECTACLE REQUIRING BOTH COURAGE AND PRECISION. Patrick's ears were ringing. The spoke of an umbrella came very close to removing his left eye. *Mary had a little lamb, little lamb, little lamb*. YES, LADIES AND GENTLEMEN, TODAY, BEFORE YOUR VERY EYES, THIS COUR-AGEOUS YOUNG MAN (pause, cheers from the crowd) *little lamb, little lamb*. THIS YOUNG MAN WILL CHALLENGE THE FURY OF NATURE, THE WRATH OF THESE HERE RAPIDS IN A VEHICLE OF HIS VERY OWN CONSTRUCTION . . . *everywhere that Mary went, Mary went, Mary went*. Patrick's mouth felt dry, his heart was pounding. The air around him smelled of the picnic lunches on the breath of the mob. A VEHICLE CALLED THE MIGHTY MOOSE MADE FROM THE HIDES AND HORNS OF THAT FINE STRONG ANIMAL KILLED BY THIS YOUNG MAN HIMSELF IN THE DARK OF OUR ANCIENT FORESTS. (More cheers, some whistles, one or two catcalls.) *Jack and Jill went up the hill*, sang Patrick's imagination, desperately. AND NOW, LADIES AND GENTLEMEN, OUR YOUNG FRIEND WILL CLIMB INSIDE HIS MIGHTY MOOSE AND WAVE GOODBYE TO YOU ALL. (Much neck craning on the part of the crowd, much waving of handkerchiefs on the part of the ladies of the crowd, more cheers.) Patrick swallowed three times in rapid succession and, running out of nursery rhymes, he began a silent repertoire of children's prayers. *Now I lay me down to sleep*. NOW, LADIES AND GENTLEMEN, AT THE SOUND OF THE GUN, THE MIGHTY MOOSE WILL BE PUSHED INTO THE THICK OF THE CRUEL

RAPIDS. ONE . . . *if I should die before I wake*, Patrick whispered, TWO . . . *I pray the Lord my soul to take*. BANG!!!

Patrick bolted through the crowd followed by angry curses of those whose view he'd blocked. He managed to get thirty or forty yards beyond the last line of spectators before he flung himself down beside some flowering shrubs. Then, the winter crowds of Bank Street, black figures on a white ground, filed through his mind and he rose and staggered further into the woods, dizzy and weak with repetitive waves of nausea. Finally, when he had gone far enough – far enough away from the smell of the crowd's damp clothing, the sausage on its collective breath, he lay quietly down on the forest floor. Rolling over on his back, he allowed the rain to fall directly on his face and the mob in his mind began to thin, the nursery rhymes to dribble away. Now there was only the sound of the rain on his forehead. The sound and the feel of it, like the day he had seen the woman under her umbrella. She had been absolutely in place, regardless of weather. Distant, serene, untouchable. So much a part of the landscape that the foliage in which she stood seemed to germinate from her. He wanted to watch her again, right now, in the wet forest – without anxiety. It did not occur to him that she would seek shelter from the weather, which would be, for her, merely a troubled stanza, something she could read, calmly, from start to finish.

He stood and began to walk along the path that lined the bank towards the tent and, as he did, the sun reappeared.

Patrick was approaching her geography without fear. She might not even see him, he reasoned, and if she did she would not know who he was, would assume that he was merely one of the spectators who, for some reason or other, had left the crowd.

When he arrived and she was not there he was neither surprised nor disappointed. Perhaps it was just the place he wanted, feeling now so weak, so disoriented. Perhaps it was just the quiet rustle of the trees she normally awoke to.

He sat near the tent, tired, calm, waiting.

By the time David returned, Patrick had been sitting outside the door of the tent for over two hours. His damp jacket, which he had removed and draped over the raised end of a log, was now almost entirely dry again. The fear connected to the crowd had left him minutes after he had arrived at the Heights and since then he had simply remained motionless in the sun, completely unaware of the alert presence of the woman on the other side of the fabric wall. His arms rested on his knees and his two hands were clasped in front of him like one oversized fist.

David pulled up a stump and sat down beside him. "He lost his head," he said to Patrick. "My God . . . it was awful."

"What happened?" asked Patrick.

"That young man from Grimsby . . . he went through those rapids and he lost his head. It was horrifying."

The crowds appeared briefly in Patrick's mind's eye and then the small floating shape between two bowler hats.

Fleda burst suddenly from the door of the tent. "Oh no," she said, "it's barbaric!"

Patrick, shocked by her unexpected materialization, jerked to his feet and backed up several paces.

"My wife," said McDougal distractedly. "Have you met?"

"No," said Fleda, nervously adjusting the mosquito netting at the entrance of the tent.

"I didn't know she was here." Patrick nodded towards the woman. "Hello," he said. God! he thought, not knowing what to do. Seeing no means of escape he sat down again on the stump and prepared to ignore her, to pretend, now that he was undeniably in her presence, that she was not there at all. Still, he was aware of her activities as she moved away from the tent. Now she was putting the kettle on the pole, now she was searching for matches, lighting the fire. She asked him if he would like some tea. He hardly replied, barely spoke to her at all, allowing her to perceive only the smallest hint of a response. He would be distant with her now. More distant than he had been when he was hidden and watching her.

David was visibly upset, could scarcely hold the cup of tea the woman placed in his hand. "I doubt you could see anything so grotesque," he said, "even in battle."

Patrick suspected that David's battles, like his own, would always take place privately, in the confines of his own mind or in the form of black marks on white paper. No mutilated bodies littering the landscape afterwards. Death would always appear in the form of a sentence for vast numbers of soldiers or as a paragraph for a particular hero.

David stirred his tea, around and around, making a small eddy in his cup. "Where did you get to anyway?" he asked Patrick. "I turned around and you had vanished."

"I was ill . . . the crowds . . . I can't . . . I thought I was through with it but . . . I couldn't function with all those people pressing in on me." Patrick rubbed his forehead with his left hand, as if he felt the pressure again, there in the woods.

Fleda glanced for a moment at the poet's hand, and at the shadow it made on his forehead. Then she looked quickly away.

No one said anything for a long time. Then David, sensing that this was a moment when one could admit to weaknesses, said to Patrick, "I probably would be no good in battle, you know."

Neither Fleda nor Patrick disagreed with him.

"All that blood, and the horses . . . suffering." He considered his own horse to be a national treasure.

"I don't care whether or not you're good in battle," said Fleda, prepared to be sympathetic, intuiting her husband's need for reassurance.

Patrick could sense that the woman's attention which, until now, he had felt hovering around himself, was sliding easily towards her husband. He felt it floating away and coming to rest in the location where it was most comfortable, and it made him briefly angry. Who *is* this woman? he wondered. This wife. He wanted to capture her somehow, to put her where she belonged in *his* story, back inside the fieldglasses where he could control the image.

The couple were beginning to discuss their plans for supper. The woman was moving in and out of the tent carrying utensils and supplies, speaking with her husband in a language that was difficult for Patrick to follow; fragmented talk, references to the small events that made up the fabric of their life together. And the objects that they handled over and over, day after day, until their intimacy with them entered a space beyond words. A mere nod of the head and the other would produce a cooking pot or a knife – it was like a sleight of hand performance. They knew each other so well, they were each other's habits. This wife, thought Patrick, this nurturer, this housekeeper!

"I will build the house here." David turned from his wife to address Patrick. He pointed to the survey stakes near the centre of the property. "And a good place for it, too, I should think, right there with the Yankees directly across the river where I can keep an eye on them."

Patrick watched the yellow ribbons on the ends of the wooden poles flicker like candles in the soft breeze.

David nodded towards his wife. "We've argued about every single aspect of it; the nature of the floorboards, the view from the windows, the size of the windows." He moved his foot back and forth, gently kicking at stones and grass. "She'd have the whole place made of windows, if possible, and the inside filled with birds and flowering plants."

Patrick smiled. He liked this version of the woman better. "I wouldn't think you'd have much trouble with the Yankees nowadays," he said.

But David did not answer. He was gone, seventy years

back ... was watching the Americans spill over the bank further down the river. Watching them spill like a dark waterfall, leap into boats and head for Queenston. Some of them had been swept so far downstream that they had to return to their own shore and begin the assault again. Some, David secretly believed, had been drowned when their boats capsized, the current still being very strong there, though nothing like the whirlpool or the rapids that led to it. And Brock. He thought of Brock, riding, riding to get there in time. Funny how he always thought of battles in terms of magnificent movement, the great seething manoeuvres of regiments, or desperate journeys on the part of commanders. Or in terms of detail. The sheen of the flank of a beautiful horse, one small heroic gesture. What he had never thought of, what he had never placed on his maps which drafted the details of endless marches, was the blood. It had simply escaped his imagination. Until right now.

Patrick began to snap small dead branches over his knee for kindling, becoming unconsciously connected to the woman's domestic chores. The sun, he noticed, was beginning to bring out pure gold highlights in her hair. It was details such as this that interested him, not her brooms and dustcloths. It would still be daylight for hours now. Summer weather. Evidence of the storm had all but disappeared. The sticks he picked up from the ground had a thin line of damp on their undersides, that was all. He placed them, dark side up, in a row by his left foot, so that they would dry.

He looked up to discover that the woman was standing directly in front of him. "I've been thinking," she said, "about the whirlpool. David told me about your swim. What made you decide to do it?"

He did not wish to hear that then. This questioning was an independent action, an act, as Patrick perceived it, of betrayal. She became again the housekeeper, completely unlike the woman he watched, the silent unconscious partner

This is what happened.

Through the small net window in the tent I saw him approach, and fear, or something like it, leapt in my heart like a fish.

I could see him approaching even though he was a long, long way off. It had been raining and then the sun came out, making everything sharper, clearer than it had been before.

The trees around him looked as if they were filled with crystal . . . tiny prisms all over the branches, and the grass he walked on was like a carpet of shattered mirrors.

Wet tree trunks, blackened by rain. I saw one of his hands there, surprisingly white, against the bark. He was steadying himself, using the tree for support.

I am trying to get this right so that I will remember. Looking through the window, looking through the mesh of netting that covers it. I know he didn't see me.

Standing entirely still, I could hear the water drop from the trees onto the canvas roof of the tent.

I saw him leave the tree and move a few steps forward. He looked directly at the tent but couldn't see me because the netting hid my face. Suddenly, I regretted that my forest did not have more pines for him. Even though I had never seen him before, I knew exactly who he was. I recognized him. He looked injured; injured and beautiful.

I thought: moving out from the door of the tent is the path that David and I have made, just since we've been here, from the tent to the fire. He was coming towards the tent, but not on that path and David wasn't with him.

When he came closer I saw that he was pale, that his clothes were soaked through, that loose twigs and leaves were attached to his jacket and trousers. I had no idea what he was going to do.

I stood so still inside the tent that I thought I might have even stopped breathing. I was so moved by the sight of this thin young man walking, almost drunkenly, through my forest . . . as if the air were difficult to move through, as if the air were water.

He didn't open the flap of the tent to look inside, but sat down on a stump instead beside the wet ashes of the fire.

I could not go out to him.

Later, when David arrived, I stepped outside, pretending that I had known nothing of the appearance of the poet. David was upset about the tragedy up the river but I couldn't concentrate on that at all, kept wondering instead what the young man was thinking, when and if he would speak to me, and what on earth I would say if he did.

His hands are beautiful . . . long and clean and pale with small blue rivers branching towards the fingers. And they are nervous, never still, running through his hair, adjusting his jacket, reaching for sticks on the ground.

I wanted to talk to him about the whirlpool, about its power. Surely he must feel it, and this must be at least part of what invites him to swim. But when I asked he seemed reluctant to answer, as if he didn't wish to speak its name.

I will never forget his approach to the tent. How hesitant it was, how tentative.

"I only knew one poet in my life
And this, or something like it, was his way"
R.B.   *As It Strikes a Contemporary*

II

For days afterwards, surprised and irritated with himself, David McDougal could not shake what he had seen. When the call for assistance had sounded over the megaphone (a mere ten minutes after the launching of The Mighty Moose), David, in his capacity as a military officer, had accompanied the doctor further along the bank, near his own property, to the whirlpool. The Old River Man was in the process of constructing a complicated series of ropes, poles, clothesline pulleys, hooks and wires, to pull the young man out of the water along with his contraption of horns and hides since the two were hopelessly and, it would appear, almost permanently intertwined. Four policemen were stationed halfway up the bank in order to discourage the stampede of spectators who were, by now, half crazy with blood-lust and curiosity.

With absolutely nothing to do until the River Man had drawn in his catch, and the possibility of very little to do after that, David looked uncomfortably across the river to the American side. There he noticed for the first time that day the dark strip of spectators lining the far shore, as if a giant mirror had been set up halfway across the river. For one moment he wondered if they had their own daredevil, their own circus to attend. But then he realized that word must have spread across the border, flushing the crowds out of their homes there as well as here. And although he had been next to certain they could see nothing at all from that distance, there they stood like a throng of pilgrims awaiting a miracle. They would be disappointed, he had suspected, angry probably, so near and yet so far from the opportunity to scrutinize injury or death. As angry as some of the men at the top of the bank who were hurling insults at the embarrassed police.

Unable to avoid it any longer, David had looked out to the centre of the whirlpool where the remains of The Mighty Moose and its passenger moved around and around like an unidentifiable beast on a strange carousel. It was difficult to determine, at this stage, which areas were beast and which were human, but there was one thing certain: neither had survived the journey in their original form. David was amazed that the two had actually remained together, the moose hide being torn to pieces. The three pairs of antlers, or at least what he could see of them, appeared to be intact, however, proving one of the young man's theories. But Buck O'Connor himself was clearly no longer in the land of the living, and bright red slashes of his blood appeared here and there on the more ordinary colour of the moose's hide, giving it, from this distance, an almost festive appearance.

The Old River Man had been guiding The Mighty Moose towards shore when David noticed the three men from the undertaking establishment descending the bank with their wicker coffin.

"How can they be so sure?" he had asked the doctor who, in turn, looked at him as if he had entirely taken leave of his senses.

Then there is nothing I can do, David had thought helplessly, there is no part for me to play. Accustomed to shouting orders, familiar with being a centre of calm in the thick of imagined chaos, he began to feel guilty about his presence at this very real disaster. As if he were just a privileged spectator with a ringside seat.

Another child.

Pneumonia.

Jas the carpenter was out in the stable covering a small, delicately carved coffin with white paint. Sam the embalmer, having already hitched up Jesus Christ and God Almighty to the wagon, was assembling his portable embalming kit, wondering, as he always did, just how he would introduce its contents (which even he admitted appeared gruesome), to the parents of the deceased. The mother was unlikely to be a problem, crazy with grief, locked in some far bedroom of the house. But several fathers had threatened to kill him if he came near their children with his equipment. Then he would just let it go, saying "Fine, fine it's your child. Of course, you know best." These were emotionally trying times for Sam. These deaths, these children. Only his loyalty to the Rochester School of Embalming persuaded him to bring along his tubes and syringes at all.

Whenever it was a child, particularly a girl, the men automatically called Maud in on the project. There were details to be worked out, details concerning ribbons and hairstyles and clothing. Hardly men's work, they felt. If the child's hair was to be in ringlets, then that was up to the mother and up to Maud. In a way it was like playing with dolls. The men hadn't been trained for it. The boys were different, little men . . . miniature copies of older corpses. Maud would be consulted then, but never expected to fix bow ties or comb hair.

Today, a little girl of five, dead in a farmhouse near Queenston. Maud, Jas, and Sam rode out there in an uncovered wagon, the little coffin, wrapped in a blanket, lying in the back. They could feel it knock the rear of the seat whenever the grade of the hill tilted downwards. They stopped only once when Jas became concerned about what this unavoidable bumping might be doing to his recently applied white finish.

The house, when they came to it, was immediately recognizable as one where a death had taken place. Dark green shades were drawn in all the windows and a black wreath decorated the rarely used front room. There was a stillness about the place, as if wind and birds had chosen, for the moment, to avoid it. Jesus Christ and God Almighty came to a gradual, dignified halt beside the front walk and waited solemnly to be tied up to the wrought-iron fence. Jas unloaded the cargo – Sam's embalming equipment and the small box – while Maud went on ahead and entered through the unpainted shed at the back of the house.

As expected, the mother was nowhere to be seen, though sobbing could be heard in another part of the house, accompanied by the low, soothing tones of a group of female comforters. The father sat motionless at the kitchen table with a few male companions, husbands, no doubt, of the chosen comforters. Maud could see that they had already consumed more than half of the bottle which stood in the centre of the table and that, on the shelf behind them, several more waited. By the end of the next three days the men would be drunk, exhausted, and surly, and the women would have regained their composure enough for severe disapproval to set in. None of this surprised Maud. She had seen it many times before.

Sam arrived in the kitchen with his embalming kit, which the father began to examine suspiciously. After an exceptionally brief conversation concerning the wonders of modern science, Sam hauled it back again to the wagon. Then he and Jas carried in the little white coffin and Maud's job began.

Two of the comforting women appeared and led Maud into the room where the little girl lay, still in her own small bed. Pneumonia, it would seem. Brown curly hair and large, fixed green eyes. Maud closed them, amazed as always, that the eyes of little girls didn't shut when you lay them down, like those of a china doll. Maud dressed the child in a green frock handed to her by one of the women. Then she tied a green ribbon in her brown hair. The dress, Maud assumed, had been chosen by the mother to match the little girl's eyes, which would be closed in the coffin, but no matter.

She laced up the little shoes, noticing that they were almost too small and were worn slightly at the heels. Still they were the child's best shoes, Maud could see that. She combed the curls, gently, carefully. No need for the hot tongs she had brought with her. The little angel's curls were natural, perfect.

Maud truly cared for her little friends, as she secretly and silently called the dead little girls during her moments of privacy with them. Little angels with their distant faces and still hands. So composed. Children caught in the centre of perfection, usually by disease, quick as lightning, so that death hardly changed them, only took away the colour from their cheeks, which Maud could replace with just a hint of rose-coloured powder. She would stay with her little friend now for the better part of three days, fixing hair, arranging flowers, going home only to sleep and, finally, just before the funeral itself, which she was never asked to attend.

On the day of the service, early in the morning, Maud would go out to her own garden to gather some of the hundreds of pansies that she grew there in the summer especially for her little friends. Then, back in the parlour of the bereaved household, she would place them all around the inside edge of the little white casket. The tiny, delicate faces of flowers . . . some company, Maud hoped, for later.

When Maud had been very small, about the size of this most recent little friend, her mother had presented her with seven or eight china dolls, carefully preserved from her own childhood. Maud had loved them all passionately . . . their little sharp teeth, their fixed shining eyes. But somehow, one way or another, she had broken them. Her mother, furious, would not from that time on allow her to own a doll. "If this farm could grow dolls," she would say, gesturing towards a hole in the barnyard where all unburnable garbage, including shattered toys, was thrown, "then you would have dolls."

On the day of the service, after she had left the bereaved household, Maud would go into the upstairs back bedroom so that she could watch the procession file into the cemetery on the hill. Jesus Christ and God Almighty, dressed in white rather than black plumes. The little white wagon with the shining glass windows. She would wait calmly at the window until she saw the mourners huddle in a circle around the grave site. Then, she would fling herself, sobbing, onto the bed. Nothing to do with death or children. Just that her beloved little friend had been taken from her; that their time together was over, forever.

Ten minutes later she would appear at her desk, perfectly composed.

That night, however, Maud would dream that the fields of her childhood farm were filled with china dolls, their faces like pansies in the distance. All of them so perfect with their little feet rooted in the ground and their little white dresses swaying in the wind. She couldn't get close to them. They always remained in the distance. No matter how fast she ran up the lane, she couldn't get close to them at all.

The following day she would find herself completely ignoring her child, treating him as if he had never been born. And he, mimicking her, would behave as if his mother had never given birth to him.

It happened that way every time.

ℐ

At first, Fleda recalled, it hadn't been quite so easy to let go of the familiar articles of domesticity. The carpet-sweeper she had owned in the old house, for instance, sometimes, even now, entered her mind like an old acquaintance – one she hadn't seen for a long time and whose face she could barely remember. And occasionally she was surprised to find earth, instead of carpets, under her feet for most of the day. True, she owned a broom, had morning chores to perform, had to sweep the tent each day, had to fill the galvanized tub with water from the barrel in order to warm it over the fire for dishes and laundry. But there was nothing here like the insistent pressure of a house that wanted putting in order. There was hardly any call to order at all.

The carpet-sweeper, she remembered, had been called "Mother's Helper," a name she found mildly ironic since she had never been, and somehow knew she would never be, a mother.

Sometimes when it was damp or cold she felt a faint sense of mourning for the old house (though never for the rooms in town), felt a sense of loss for its calm, quiet, predictable rooms, and the furniture that filled them. Then she would wander through her old home in her imagination, taking note of its eccentricities, its bric-a-brac, the piano, the view from the window over the sink, until at last she came to the spot she had called The Poet's Corner, the location of much pleasure and much disquietude.

There she had placed engraved portraits of her favourite writers on the wall, and copies of their books on a table beneath, a kind of shrine where, in true religious form, she could leave behind the perceived world. As David spent more and more time in his study untangling the mysteries of his battles, she spent more and more time with these other men, until the hallucination of their language, the strength of their fantasies became, at times, more real to her than the man whose meals she cooked, whose socks she darned.

Then the house became a kind of fortress where she sequestered herself with these companions, with their visions, their dark landscapes, until she knew the geography of Venice, of Florence, of the English Lake District, better than the streets of Fort Erie, the hotels of Niagara Falls. No church bazaar, no meeting of the Ladies' Auxiliary could pull her from their influence. The women of the area became suspicious and, as she became more aloof from them, finally angry and cruel. The men were simply frightened. In another era she might have been burned at the stake.

Then came her husband's posting to Niagara, the sale of the house, the storage of the furniture, and the removal to temporary quarters in Kick's Hotel. The second that Fleda had closed the door for the last time, had heard the latch drop and the lock click, she knew it was the end of a period, a cycle. She took her books with her into the real landscape of her own country.

From then on, except in those rare moments when she mourned the old place, her home became a dream, a piece of imaginary architecture whose walls and windows existed in the mind and therefore could be rearranged at will. A house where the functions of rooms changed constantly, where a wing could be added or a staircase demolished, where furniture could re-upholster itself, change shape, size, period.

Today, gazing past David's socks, which she had hung on a branch to dry, she watched the ribbons on the survey stakes move in the summer breeze, still cool at this hour, and knew, for her, there would be no actual house, not soon, not ever. The stakes marked out a dream, an illusion, which if laboured into permanence, would produce a similar fortress and the feeling of caged torpor she was now beginning to associate with her last dwelling. She walked over to the space that she and David had carefully paced out and, on impulse, swung her arm right through the spot where the library windows ought to have been, feeling the cold, free air on her wrist as she did so. Then, stepping lightly over the string which connected the stakes, she began to walk right through the non-existent walls.

She had broken out of the world of corners and into the organic in a way that even her beloved poets in their cottages and villas hadn't the power to do, and the acre had become her house. The acre and the whirlpool. Predictable flux, entry and exit of animals, birds, cloud formations, phases of the moon. The arrival and departure of men, returning to their rooms, to rectangles and corners, while she breathed whirlpool and kept her place there and her fire. The tent functioned for her merely as a shelter. And, unlike a real house, it was capable of motion and response; sagging a bit after a storm, billowing and flapping in the wind.

She was standing where the kitchen should have been, her body immersed in a transparent pantry cupboard, when Patrick took up a final, permanent residence in her mind. The poet. Released from boundaries, from rectangles, basements, attics, floors and doors, she felt free to allow him access, whatever form that access might take. Every cell in her body, every synapse in her brain, demanded the presence of the poet in her life. As if all the reading, all the dreaming, had been one long preparation for his arrival.

His arrival, which coincided so neatly with her departure. Departure from everything she had assumed she would be; from the keeping of various houses, from the sameness of days lived out inside the blueprint of artificially heated rooms, from pre-planned, rigidly timed events – when this happened in the morning and that happened in the afternoon, just because it always had and always would.

Fleda walked over to the tent and opened its soft door easily with the back of her hand. The mosquito netting clung for a moment to one of her shoulders then dropped comfortably back into place. Then, moving her fingers through skeins of wool and spools of thread in her sewing basket, she soon grasped cold steel. Holding the blades downwards for safety, she took the scissors with her to the outdoors and placed them on a stump in the sunlight where they shone with an unusual, almost foreign, brilliance. Then she began to pull the pins out of the bun at the back of her neck.

As she cut her long, long hair to a spot just below her shoulders, she remembered the years it had taken her to grow it; how, since she had been an adult, there had always been the morning problem of doing up her hair and how that problem would exist no longer. The act of cutting her hair now was difficult and required strength as it was thick and often resisted the blades. She managed, however by separating it into six parts as her mother always had when she braided it for school. The severed portions Fleda paid no attention to whatsoever, merely flung them to the wind or onto the ground. Finishing, she brushed off her skirt, and the part of her back she could reach, and decided to walk down the path to the whirlpool.

She hadn't gone more than twenty steps down the bank when she remembered the scissors and, wanting to return them to her work basket, she changed her direction.

Then she saw Patrick and stopped.

The poet, darkly dressed, his back bent, collecting her discarded hair; stuffing first the pockets of his trousers and then his jacket with it, moving from place to place, chasing the strands that were beginning to be carried away by the wind.

Gradually Fleda understood that he had watched her before, and often, and the knowledge both frightened and delighted her. "How wonderful this is," she whispered to herself as she moved quietly away so that he would not see her. "To think that he looks at me."

As she was returning from the whirlpool later that afternoon, she thought about her husband's gifts to her. Books and books and now, finally, the poet himself in the flesh. Patrick, with the long sensitive hands and pale skin, his reddish hair surrounding his head like a burning aura. The weak, long, listless body. To think that he had crept through the woods like an intruder, a ghost, a witness, responding, and now he had crept right up to the hearth rug of a dream which had spilled through walls and into the landscape.

Fleda sighed and unconsciously walked right through the spot where the front door of the house was to be, heading back, once again, to the tent. Inside she picked up a plaid blanket and reached towards Patrick's small book which David had brought only a few days before to the forest. Then, disturbed by the emotions that the sight of the little collection aroused in her, she changed her mind, felt that examining its contents, at this moment, would be an invasion of privacy, though whose she was not entirely sure. She glanced at the bed where she and David had spent the night, noticing the jumble of an unsmoothed blanket which looked as if it might have concealed an oddly shaped beast. Then, after running her fingers once over the embossed book cover, she left the poems unopened on the pine table.

Outside again, she walked over to the section of the bank where the whirlpool was visible, despite thick foliage. There she placed herself in the hammock which David had strung between two cedars. For a minute or two she looked down, watching the few seagulls who had ventured this far inland from the lake move around and around, following the pattern of the current. For the first time she felt the several parts of her world interlock . . . felt herself a part of the whirlpool, a part of the art of poetry.

&

Every weekday morning, around eleven o'clock, Sam joined Maud in the kitchen to drink coffee, discuss business, and gossip. Nowadays, the child was usually present at these meetings, listening intently, as if he were consciously building his vocabulary.

As the kitchen did not face south like the sunroom, it was not filled with the same kind of overpowering light. Still, there was a warm feeling to it, pine being the predominant material used in the chairs, tables, and cupboards in the room. Maud, herself, lightened the atmosphere now that she was no longer in full mourning. She had changed her entire wardrobe to mauves, and light mauves at that, moving as close as she could to the edge of half-mourning while still maintaining her respectability. Today, she looked almost pretty, dressed in a lavender calico cotton print with a bit of white lace at the throat and the sleeves. The brooch containing Charles' hair looked decorative rather than sombre when pinned on this costume.

Sam was concerned about Jesus Christ, his favourite of the two horses.

"She just doesn't seem to have much pep," he said to Maud. "Nothing like the way she used to be. I remember two or three years back you'd dress her up for a funeral and she'd just know she was going on parade."

"Parade, par-ade," the child echoed.

"She'd hold her head up like a queen, shake her feathers. Now she's just listless, like she just doesn't care any more. I think she is depressed about something."

"Something," the child announced.

"Remember," said Maud, "she's not as young as she used to be. She's been here a long, long time. Maybe we should be looking for a new horse."

"God Almighty would go into conniptions if we replaced her," said Sam, alarmed. "I don't think he could work with anyone else."

"Connip-tions," the child repeated, and then, because it was such a strange, new word, he repeated it again.

"Used to be," Sam continued, "you'd put her in a military funeral and she'd just fire right up. She likes music, you know, especially marching bands. She likes those drums and she was never frightened of the salute like some horses might be. God Almighty, now, he would sometimes get a little nervous, but never Jesus. She'd just stand there at attention, like the soldiers."

"Gun!" exclaimed the child, and Maud smiled at him, pleased that he had made the connection.

"How was it?" she asked Sam, referring to the funeral a few days earlier, of the last 1812 veteran in the neighbourhood.

"Just fine," said Sam. "That historian went on and on with his address, but apart from that it was just fine. Except for Jesus being listless."

"*List*less," said the child, and this time his little face mirrored Sam's worried expression.

Sam and Maud drank their coffee silently for a while, mindful of the child's seeming ability to totally digest their conversations. The child got down from his stool and walked over to the sink where he discovered an empty cup. Soon, he was back at the table, pretending to drink coffee along with the adults.

"That was the strangest thing," Sam eventually said.

"You mean the horse?" asked Maud.

"No, no, that other funeral."

"Oh ... the stunt man's."

"No, remember last week when Peter and I took the casket to Chippewa?"

Maud nodded. The child nodded.

"Well, we get there, and here is this young girl, lying in bed, dead as a doornail from TB." Sam stood up, walked over to the stove, poured himself a second cup of coffee, and returned to the table. "There she was," he continued, "and pretty too. You know how some of them aren't if they've been sick too long, even if they were to begin with."

Maud crossed her arms and nodded again.

"Well, this one has a wedding dress laid out over her, on top of the blankets, with the veil on her head, partly covering her face."

"What ... why?" asked Maud.

"Seems she was engaged to the grocer's son when she took sick and her dress and all was all made up and then when they knew for certain she was going to die, her mother decides she'd better get married first." Sam looked thoughtfully down into his coffee cup.

Maud waited for him to continue.

"So they called in the parson and, because by then the girl was too weak to put on the gown, they just laid it on top of her on the bed and put the veil on her and married her up."

"Oh no ..." said Maud.

"And then she just immediately died. Just like that, right under her wedding dress."

Maud shook her head. "Oh no ..." said the child.

"It is strange to be dying and getting married at exactly the same time," said Sam. "The mother even decides that she has to wear the wedding dress in the casket. And now, because she's dead and not just weak, she can put her right inside it."

"Married," said the child. "Dying."

"So then, when Peter and I go back there three days later for the funeral, to take her to church, you know, the mother's got all these pretty dresses . . . all different colours, all laid out like, all over the furniture in the parlour. Seems they belonged to the bride. And what does the mother do but start rolling them up and stuffing as many as she can into the coffin with the girl. 'She'll need her trousseau,' she kept on saying, 'She'll need her trousseau.'"

"Trou-sseau," said the child.

Sam was silent for several moments. Then he spoke. "Not much upsets me, but that bride did. And maybe that's what upset Jesus Christ too. Her pulling that bride with all her clothes packed around her, down to the church and then over to the graveyard. Horses have feelings, you know. Maybe that bride upset her."

"Bride," the child whispered to himself, liking the sound of the word. "Bride, bride."

Maud carried Sam's story around with her for the rest of the day, thinking about costumes. Lord, she thought, they are always dressing you up as something and then you are not yourself anymore. This young girl, the frozen, immobilized bride, coerced into it and then dead and unable to ever grow beyond it. No one now would even remember her name. Anecdotally, she would always be the bride, the one who was married and buried in the same breath.

Just as Maud in her costume of violet cotton would still be "the widow," were she to stop now.

Bride, wife, widow. She would not stop now.

⁂

27 July, 1889

David has informed me that rattlesnakes have been spotted hereabouts so now I seem to anticipate reptilian shapes flickering at the edge of my vision. I have been unable to ascertain whether they rattle before or after they strike, but will hope that it is before. Funny that the sound of a child's toy should be a portent of doom.

Patrick spent the morning here with us in an endless and unsuccessful search for a tiny wild orchid called Ladies' Tresses, which he says blooms only around the U.S./Canadian border. He has a small botany book, which he now carries everywhere, and fieldglasses for the birds. We descended the bank through the damp, leafy places where the plant should have existed, but found absolutely none, only a great deal of fireweed. David says the Americans probably stole every example. I had my umbrella with me though the sun was shining. I swung it through the undergrowth in front of me to flush out rattlers, but we found none of those either.

Patrick said only six words to me all day, in the form of a question: "Why have you brought your umbrella?"

He didn't stay to hear my answer but rushed on ahead, eager to get to the whirlpool.

It is becoming more and more difficult. How much of this am I imagining and how much is real? Does he intentionally make metaphoric reference to his own behaviour . . . looking for Ladies' Tresses? I am sure, or, at least I think I am sure, that he still watches me. I have seen the glimmer of his fieldglasses in the forest, and once I glimpsed his tweed jacket through the leaves. Then, when he's here we behave with such indifference towards each other. And David carrying on about the war as if nothing were happening. Nothing is happening.

And yet . . . and yet, I feel the power of his observation.

I think of "Andrea del Sarto." Why did Browning put the cousin's whistle at the end of the poem? Perhaps it should have been there throughout. Every time I read the poem I hear the sound of it from the beginning; a subtle invitation – come out from behind your walls into the scenery. Let the view change around you . . . forever. And Andrea:

> *"the weak-eyed bat no sun should tempt*
> *Out of the grange whose four walls make his world."*

Andrea imagining heaven as "Four great walls in the New Jerusalem."

Earlier this evening, just before dark, I walked out into the night air, over to the edge of the bank. Quarter moon over the whirlpool. Quite abruptly, just at the moment when it's not quite night, the sky opened, exposed its black distances. Everything around me became unsurveyed . . . unsurveyable.

Now, searching for a voice other than the dark, I am back in the tent reading. Here the coal-oil lamp on the table turns the canvas yellow-orange and deepens the odd bits of colour on the furniture.

In this light I am reading Browning. Pulling in around Browning, trying to avoid the pull of the open dark, the limitlessness of the stars over the whirlpool.

Reading Browning. Learning Patrick.

"Love's corpse lies quiet therefore
Only love's ghost plays truant
And warns us how in wholesome awe
Durable masonry; that's wherefore
I weave but trellis-work pursuant
— Life, to law"

Part of me, however, still listens to the night; not to the small intimate sounds, scratching and rustling near the tent, but to the larger experiences: the low, constant sigh of the whirlpool, the gentle, steady breeze at the top of the pines.

I am listening and reading, my attention shifting from Browning to the outdoors, to a glimmer of Patrick, back to Browning. And once, after I had read the lines:

"The solid, not the fragile
Tempts the rain and hail and thunder"

I was certain that I could hear the creaking of a thousand stars as they changed position in that dark, unfathomable sky.

*

August in the garden. Maud was engrossed in weed removal, making room for the late-summer blossoms, tending the precious beds of pansies. Wind high in the maples at the front of the building, breezes closer to the ground.

Maud looked at the child. He was so beautiful there in the garden in mid-August, his fair hair illuminated by sun and moving gently on the current of the air.

"Lovely boy," she said quietly, brushing a lock of golden hair out of his eyes.

"Lovely boy," he replied, ignoring her caress.

The garden gloves made her hands look like two small kittens curled on the pattern of her apron. She rested for a moment, kneeling on the grass, shadows of leaves on her hands, her shoulders.

Maud sensed the chrysanthemums of early autumn stirring, twitching their roots below the ground. Everywhere on the grass there was light and darkness, moving and changing. Beside her lay a collection of dead, discardable blossoms. Sweet odour of decay.

She was wearing her mauve cotton dress and had opened it at the collar to let the breeze touch her throat. Inside the gloves her hands were ringless, all jewellery left behind in the house. Happy, absorbed in her activities, she began to sing. A thin sound, carried all over the garden by the wind.

The child moved towards the picket fence that separated the front yard from the street. "Man," he said, very quietly, under his breath.

Maud stopped singing. She assumed that he was referring to the small tree he stood directly in front of.

"No," she said, from force of habit. "Bush."

"*The* man," said the boy, louder this time, gazing past the pickets out into the empty thoroughfare.

"The road?" questioned Maud. "Don't you mean the road?"

It was so dry in this season that tiny whirlwinds of dust moved up Main Street borne on the back of the breeze. The child watched one of these make its irregular progress past the front gate.

"The man," he said again.

Maud pushed her spade into the arid soil and rose slowly to her feet. She walked over to the spot where the child was standing and, placing one hand on his shoulders, scrutinized his line of vision, noticing the whirlwind as she did so.

"Dust," she said emphatically.

"The man," replied the child, searching up and down the street.

"The man?" asked Maud, and then, speaking mostly to herself, "What man? There is no man."

"There is no man," mimicked the boy. He was silent, serious for a few moments. Then he began again.

"Where is this man?" asked Maud. "There's no man here. Who is this man? Why are you talking about a man? Flower," she said, drawing his attention towards a yellow rose.

"The man," said the boy, entirely disregarding the flower.

"All right," said Maud, resigned. "The man."

The child's small face lit up like a lamp. "Oh," he said, looking at his mother. "Oh, the man."

What was this, Maud wondered; why, now, this repetitive word?

"Oh," responded the boy. "Oh, the man." He paused. "Swim," he said.

Maud turned abruptly back to the garden, tired, so tired of arbitrary words.

"Forest," the child said, following her to the flower-bed, his features filled with animation.

"No!" said Maud, suddenly straightening her spine and shaking her head, these disembodied nouns making her oddly uncomfortable. "No more of this today." She waved the child away. "No more words," she said. "In fact," she continued, "no more sounds."

"The man," said the boy sadly as he turned away from his mother.

Maud removed seven weeds in rapid, angry succession, then sat back on her heels as if waiting for the garden to grow, or for a flower to unfurl before her very eyes, to show her, in an immediate way, that some of her efforts produced results. Nothing, of course, changed at all.

It seemed to her that only in her absence could miraculous transformations occur; only while she slept or lapsed into forgetfulness. Then the river released its dead, the child spoke, her garden blossomed, the season changed. But never under her direct gaze. A phrase ... the man ... had slipped into the child's mind. Where had she been when that happened?

As she raked the earth with her garden tools she relaxed, forgetting, and began to sing again. Soon she heard the child, his voice mingling with her own. Singing too, perhaps. Then she heard the words rise above her own voice.

"O my God, my God!" he wailed in a shrill woman's voice. "What am I going to do? What am I going to do?"

He had made a tiny burial mound out of the garden dirt. The chief mourner, he was a woman hysterical. The sound of pure female grief filled the garden coming, it seemed, from each direction until Maud covered her ears to be through with it.

The child was rocking back and forth by the little toy grave, sunlight and shadow dancing all over the grass.

$\mathscr{D}$

Fleda was haunted, almost constantly now, by the idea of the poet watching her. She was fascinated, and as her fascination grew it began to surround her like a bubble, a bubble she couldn't break. She would be sitting by the fire or clearing weeds with David, who would be talking about *his* museum, *his* book when suddenly the other man's name would slip out of her mind and into the conversation; softly, easily, like a knife entering butter. She began to question her husband.

"What do you and Patrick talk about?"

"Do you think he's found anything to write about here?"

Whole scenes in which the poet had played a part would superimpose themselves over her present landscape until Fleda felt she could only really reach her husband by swimming through a foggy dream of Patrick. A clump of today's poplars on her right was blocked by a memory of the time she had cut her hair and Patrick had stuffed his pockets full of it. The noise of the axe against the cedar tree David was now chopping ... eliminated by a scene from the whirlpool: Patrick observing the currents, the swimmer in him active, alive.

He was not the dark man she had dreamed about during her childhood, not the one who arrived one morning and obliterated the past with his passion.

The past remained unaltered, strong behind this curtain, this veil of recent memory. The afternoon Patrick had read Swinburne's "Triumph of Time" aloud, slowly, dreamily. The morning he had arrived at their acre early, crazy after nightmares, with his red hair uncombed, electrified. Fleda had decided, then, to tell him about the veil he was creating, the one that separated her from the present.

"I imagine . . ." she had begun.

"The imagination is a trap," he had interrupted, looking at her sideways, running his fingers through his hair, then looking away, always looking away.

He hadn't wanted to hear it, whatever it was she was going to say.

It astonished her how quickly these moments became memory. In the morning he would be with them, talking or not talking, walking or sitting by the fire. And then, later in the day, the whole episode would present itself over and over in her imagination; a memory, a fear, a mood she couldn't shake, placing a curtain between her and whatever else was happening. Often, she caught herself talking to him when he wasn't there; quietly, through her teeth as if in anger, saying the same words in whispered imagination that she had said only a few hours before in reality. And he, she suspected, back at the farm, not writing, thinking about the whirlpool. And she, near the whirlpool, not reading the poems he had already written.

And then her terrible urge to interpret, until even the most ordinary conversation became allegorical.

"I used to call this part Windy Poplars," she had said, pointing to an area of land near the bank, "but now I've changed the name."

"What would you like to call it now?" he had asked, almost as if he were aware that since his arrival the names of everything had changed.

But she hadn't answered, knowing that their conversation

had suddenly nothing whatsoever to do with a spot of grass surrounded by trees.

But, perhaps, she had thought later, when the scene, their conversation, was presenting itself over and over in her mind, perhaps he didn't understand at all, the fractured context of these references she unconsciously made. Hadn't she, after all, begun with the intention of talking about trees?

These fractured memories all around her when he wasn't there, became stronger and stronger the longer he was gone until, if she hadn't seen him for several days, they *were* the present and she could hardly recognize his face when it appeared, talking from behind the veil.

"Where are you, Fleda?" David would ask.

"It's this spot," she answered, "making me dreamy."

True, landscape might have been able to accomplish that. Still, in reproductions of famous Italian pictures that she had looked at, it was the figure dominating the landscape that caught the attention, held the memory.

Fleda wondered if Patrick's intended swim was an attempt to confront and thereby purify the landscape, to erase his fear of the strange magnetic pull of the whirlpool. If he swam it, would he cease to regard it with awe? And might he then be able to approach *her* openly?

The idea attracted her. She imagined him, successful, climbing the bank, coming right towards her.

How had this man, who she hardly knew, entered her world and caused all the names to change?

She looked out at her acre now from behind the walls of a bubble of glass that had grown around her, a curtain of memory that had fallen between her and the place where she lived.

II

The Old River Man appeared at the screen door with a package, something damp, wrapped in brown paper. He had taken the long way around the garden, having noted that Jesus Christ and God Almighty, of whom he was deeply afraid, were outside of the stable, hitched up to the wagon. Horses were such large and obvious beasts of the earth, so foreign to water, that he would go miles out of his way to avoid them. Now, he stood at the screen door, clutching his parcel, looking nervously over his shoulder, checking to make sure the horses weren't coming any closer.

Maud, who happened to be in the kitchen then, scowled at him from somewhere near the stove. Babies, sometimes even babies. Maud had no time for babies. She had told him over and over to leave the babies in the river. No one will claim them, she said, they are nobody's children.

These babies were not like her little friends with their lovely little hands and feet. These were unwanted extensions of other women's bodies.

"It's not a baby," the old man said now, aware of Maud's frown.

She pushed open the door and walked outside to speak to him. The Old River Man stepped a few paces back and, after once again turning to note the location of the horses, he placed the parcel on the ground in the shadow of a clump of Shasta daisies.

Within minutes Maud was writing:

> *Right arm of a man*
> *no marks to lead to positive identification*
> *except tattoo*
> *says, "Forget me not, Annie"*
> *surrounded by a heart-like shape.*

So far that season, that spring and summer, there had been seventeen "floaters" for Maud to deal with. She knew precisely what it meant each time the Old River Man appeared at her back door under her defunct porch lamp. Their conversations, at these moments, were limited, almost ritualistic. Cap in hand, smelling of river, his hip-waders shining with moisture, he would wait for her to speak.

"Where?"

To this question there were only two possible answers: Maid of the Mist Landing or down by the whirlpool. It depended on the original location of the drowning and the currents of the river. At a certain place beyond the falls a decision was made by the water, some of which moved to the left, over to the dock, while the rest moved towards the lower rapids and eventually into the whirlpool. Left at the mercy of this kind of chance, the human remains ended their journey in either the former or the latter location, though, on certain occasions, if the trip had been particularly rough, they might end up in both.

Once the Old River Man had relayed his information, he would shift uneasily from foot to foot while his eyes slid to the corner cupboard where he knew his payment (in the form of a seemingly endless supply of Seagram's whiskey) was kept. Then, bottle in hand, he would disappear through a break at the end of the garden. This time the child had witnessed the close of the meeting and, looking directly at his mother, had said the word "whirlpool" in the River Man's gravelly voice.

Within a matter of a few weeks the child had become a perfect mimic, repeating not only every word spoken but reproducing the tone, the pitch of the voice as well. Maud had to believe now that through the years that he had remained stubbornly silent, he had been digesting, verbatim, conversations, arguments, and harangues. And that he had been listening carefully (perhaps through the grates in the floor) to the funeral preparations, the carpenter's chatter, the long, hysterical monologues of those who came to Grady and Son to choose a coffin for someone they loved.

Now, at least once a day, the child would repeat the whole performance: the sobs of the widow, Sam's artificial condolences, the sales pitch, his voice adopting the tone of the speaker. After she had repeatedly tried and failed to interrupt the process, Maud found herself attempting to guess whose funeral he was playing back to her, as if she were involved in some form of tasteless parlour game. As she bent over her needlework and the child chattered, or whispered, or shouted in the corner, she would find herself commenting mentally, "Why that must have been Jake Warner's," or "That sounds like Mrs. Simpson after she lost her daughter Ella." Then, shocked at her own complacency, she would cross the room, get down on her knees, and beg the child to stop, only to be answered by an exact reproduction of her own entreaty.

He was unpredictable. Sometimes he would go for days repeating only a word here and there.

"I'm going downstairs now," Maud would say.

"Now," the child would repeat.

Then, the next day he would break, quite suddenly, into a chorus of one of the embalmer's lewd songs and in the embalmer's tenor voice.

This turn of events began to affect all conversation at Grady and Son. Maud dared not discuss the neighbours' activities with Sam for fear their words might be repeated during a friendly visit. This eliminated gossip. The child was light on his feet, moved like a cat. You never knew when he might be listening, or how far the sound of your own voice might travel. Slowly, but inevitably, the reversal took place. The child spoke constantly, his mother and her employees hardly at all.

Once, after a lengthy and gruelling interview with the relatives of a man who was drowned and buried, unidentified, some weeks before, Maud heard the child speaking in her voice in the evening, from deep in the darkness of his bedroom. He was reciting the same list she had recited to them. Hearing him, she was disturbed by the clipped, professional sound of her voice, cold, removed. "Apparently dark complexioned," the voice stated, "thumb and finger on left hand disfigured, light woollen underdrawers, upper teeth good, eyes apparently brown."

Unable, finally, to hear it any longer, she threw open the door to his room with such force that the doorknob made an indentation in the adjacent plaster wall.

"Why?" she demanded. "Why are you doing this? You must stop, immediately, now, you must stop!"

"Stop!" the child shouted.

The sound of her own voice coming back to her, from the other side of the room.

The child borrowing her voice, shouting, "STOP, STOP, STOP, STOP!"

Some summers the river was possessive of its dead and kept the flesh to itself. Then the Old River Man appeared at the back door only three or four times during the season, occasionally with news only of fragments. Maud could never understand it; a season with twenty-nine or thirty river bodies followed by one with only two or three, and no obvious changes in the condition of humanity or the weather. But the Old River Man showed no surprise – only vague disappointment that the catch had been so small. He called these "dry summers," more because of his lack of remuneration than with any reference to the river itself. But this year there had been a bumper crop and the old man was drunk most of the time, so much so that Maud began to worry that the whiskey might affect his ability to spot the drowned and battered flesh. Nonetheless he arrived with regularity, displaying only a slight stagger when he moved away again towards the end of the garden.

Maud was paid fifteen dollars per body by the city, in return for disposing quickly and quietly of these unpleasant embarrassments to the mighty tourist industry. The flesh itself did not bother her. She could hardly refer to it, in its condition, as human. It had changed beyond that, had become, instead, some other kind of element. It was the objects and bits of apparel that this flesh had attached to itself on the last day of its existence that both disturbed and fascinated her. And it was these things that she recorded and kept, though she knew that they were not destructible like the body, unless put to death by something stronger than water, something like fire. When she examined, and then began to list the contents of pockets, she was forced to remember that the thing before her, packed in ice, had been human ... stupid, self-deluding, vain, tender. Then the questions would enter her mind and a relationship would form between her and the drowned flesh. A personality would develop behind the words, a life would take shape.

Why had this flesh dressed itself on the morning of its death? Why the choice of blue socks, or a blue tie-pin? Why the coins in the pocket, the rabbit's foot, a *good luck* charm, religious medals around necks destined for annihilation, watches recording the exact moment of contact with the water, rings with their precious stones missing, eyeglasses in the breast-pocket of a suit coat? Why the suit coat at all, when your destination is the river, the rocks?

The answers to these questions, which were not answers at all, mere speculations, built a frail network of history around each death. Maud's collection of private legends, stored verbally in her notebook and concretely in her cupboard at the end of the hall. This was how she maintained order, how she gathered together some sense out of the chaos of the deaths around her.

As she closed her book after making a record of the tattooed arm, she recalled the sound of the child's voice travelling through the garden.

"What am I going to do? What am I going to do?"

His little voice, high and cracking in a bizarre parody of female sorrow.

I Last night Patrick suggested that we play hearts.
Rain over the whirlpool and no fire to inspire
talks about battles and nationalism. Overcast and dark
early – no celestial spectacles to discuss. So we were
trapped, by lamplight, inside the tent.

Patrick suggested that we play hearts and then, I'm
sure, looked momentarily in my direction from his position
at the opposite side of the table. David, used to playing
poker at the camp, had never familiarized himself with the
rules of this game. I had never played cards in my life.

When three play (and I was eventually pressed into join-
ing them), one must discard the two of spades before beginning. This, from Patrick, who seemed to know much about
these games. He went on to say that it is customary for the
eldest hand to lead. We all knew who that was.

I was in charge of all the shuffling and dealing, Patrick
insisting that I should deal to the right, thereby allowing
David the first card and me the responsibility of giving it to
him.

The sole object of the game, Patrick informed me, was to
rid yourself of all the hearts you may possess, because he

who ends up with the most is, oddly enough, the loser, not the winner.

One aims, in this game, for the lowest possible score, and the highest card of any suit takes the trick.

David foolishly placed an ace of hearts, worth fourteen points, on the table at the very beginning of the game.

Patrick, knowing David would now have to take all, slapped a knave of hearts on top of it.

I added a ten, my highest card in suit.

At one point, when David had no clubs, he gave Patrick, who took that particular trick, the queen of hearts.

I won, finishing with not a single heart, not a single point. Patrick came in second. David lost dramatically, managing to assemble, on his side of the table, almost every heart in the deck.

Patrick was finding new ways to look at her – shadows and reflections. Once, while he was toying with a spoon, he had captured her face in it and had held it there while she, unaware, had continued to read a book. Once, for several moments, he had watched her reflected in her husband's eyes. Tonight, while they played cards, he observed her head and shoulders as they appeared in the globe of a coal-oil lamp.

When the game was over, he walked to the opposite side of the tent. Picking up Fleda's hand mirror, he adjusted it so that he could see her even though his back was turned. He could see all of her although she could see only his eyes in the mirror.

"You won," he said to Fleda, not turning around.

She lowered her gaze, away from the strange, disembodied eyes in the mirror. "Yes, perhaps."

The wind picked up, shaking the canvas walls around them.

Fleda's eyes snapped back to the mirror he was holding. "Patrick," she said. "Patrick . . . turn around."

He stood motionless with the mirror in his hand.

"Patrick, please turn around."

He placed the mirror back on the washstand and turned to face her. He is looking at me, she thought, as though I were an eclipse, too dangerous to be perceived directly.

"Patrick," she continued, pulling herself out from the magnetic field he was creating, "are you going to persist with your idea about swimming?"

"Yes, I will be swimming soon. I believe you understand why."

She thought she understood but wondered if he did. How much longer could she continue to play his vague, illusive games? Again, she had the feeling that they were discussing two subjects at once, or was it all the same thing?

"Maybe you could accomplish what you want by just watching it," Fleda said.

"No, that's not enough."

"Why isn't it?"

"Why isn't watching the forest enough for you?" asked Patrick, turning the question back towards the woman.

Fleda became flushed, embarrassed. After all, this was really the most they had ever spoken to each other. "What is it that you want to prove?"

"What are you trying to prove living out here in the woods?"

"What does that matter?"

"It matters to me."

Yes, thought Fleda. She remembered the day when she had stood under her black umbrella, looking down towards the whirlpool. She knew now that she had seen Patrick there, so far away that he would not have been recognizable. He must have been watching her, even then.

"Patrick," she said softly, and then stopped. She could see David out of the corner of her eye, watching, listening to the progression of their conversation.

"What is it," she eventually asked, "that you want?"

Patrick reached for his walking stick. Was she trying to deny him the whirlpool? "I thought," he said quietly, "that you might see this, or at least you might try to." He opened the canvas door of the tent. "Goodnight, David," he said as he stepped out into the darkness.

The tent flap fell back into place. Fleda walked across the planking to her husband, then changed her mind. Moving swiftly to the table, she grabbed the lantern.

"He'll need some light," she told David as she hurried out of the tent.

Outside, she caught up to him easily. "Here," she said thrusting the lantern into his hand. "I really do care, you know. What you think is important to me." She grabbed his other hand with her own. "Patrick," she said, pulling on his unresponsive arm. "I want to understand this."

He faced her now, directly, in the circle of light. How strange she looked; shadows around her eyes, light on her cheekbones.

"Please tell me why you want to do it," Fleda persisted, but quietly, coaxing, wanting him to speak to her.

This light I'm holding, he thought, makes everything not directly in its path much darker. He stood, silent with her, in the path of the light.

"How can you want me to understand and not tell me?"

"It's just swimming," he said softly.

"Oh no," she said, "no, it isn't. Nothing is just this or that anymore. Everything means something else . . . doesn't it?"

"Does it?" he asked, looking towards the dark. "Yes . . . I suppose it does."

The wind began to rise in earnest. It moved the flame under the glass in the lantern so that the shadows of the man and the woman leapt into elongation and shrank again, suddenly, on the forest floor.

General Brock's hat had disturbed the major for years. How could a man, even such a man, have a head that large? It suggested weird tumours or water on the brain. It suggested to Major David McDougal that Brock had a swelled head. Moreover there was something else absurd about it. It had not arrived in time.

It had not arrived in time to be on the general's head when he either foolishly or, as David would have it, heroically, rushed up Queenston Heights, shouting, "'Push on, brave York Volunteers!'" It was still somewhere in transit, having been ordered from England. Neither the hat nor its impressive box showed any sign of battle. Its plume shot up, like a tiny fountain, from a black and red surface. A perfect target, but one that had never been used.

Now the coat . . . the coat was worn, dirty, and contained the fatal bullet hole. Dead centre in the chest. No one could possibly survive that. Tiny perfect death hole, blood camouflaged by red worsted material, brass buttons shuddering in the final throes.

He had seen the coat in Ottawa, but here they had only the hat.

David was standing in front of a mahogany case which was one of many crowded into a third-storey room above the courthouse. The historical room. Masses of objects crammed into a closed space. The hat shared a case with a Roman battle axe that had been found in an Ayrshire bog, and any number of Indian arrowheads, and Miss Wilmot's grandmother's collection of pressed flowers from Wales.

David desperately wanted a pure museum ... one where he could place the relics of the thin history of the country where he lived. In his rooms he had a small pile of cannon-balls given to him by the woman in the funeral home. She had found bullets too, she said, and buttons, but had no idea where they were. Part of the battlefield was now her garden, the other part the graveyard and the orchard. She had been kind, had allowed him to wander out in the garden as long as he liked, searching the grass for signs.

He heard his wife move at the end of the room, somewhere near the needlework section. He could hear her skirts moving across the planked floor. Suddenly she was speaking to him.

"David, come with me for a moment." They walked to the opposite side of the room. "Have you seen this?" She was using the tone of voice, low, almost frightened, that people adopt in museums and picture galleries.

She was pointing to a small appliquéd quilt which hung on the wall above the marine exhibit. Although the silk and velvet which had been pieced together were beginning to shred, the colours were still vibrant enough to play against each other. Embroidery surrounded the various shapes, and at the bottom was worked into a date ... 1813. Of a strange size, it was meant to hang on the wall, unlikely to have ever been used as a coverlet.

"It's lovely," David said to his wife.

"But don't you see what it is?"

He looked again, into the decorative geometric design, a pattern moving towards a centre.

"A quilt," he announced. "There are several others near the door, if you are interested."

"But David, look at the graveyard." She pointed to a square area in the centre surrounded by a fabric fence. "And here – " she swept her hand around the edge – "here is a border of coffins, each with a name."

David leaned forward a little. "In some spots they are missing."

"That's because they have been taken to the graveyard."

David moved even closer to the object until he could see evidence of missing stitches in the spot where the coffins had been removed, had been taken into the velvet graveyard.

"My God," he whispered, "Why on earth. . . ?"

"Why not?" Fleda turned to look directly at him. "Why not?" How could all this sewing be any worse than the reality of – "

"But it's so calculated, as if this woman knew that everybody was going to die."

"Everybody is going to die."

"But it's almost as if she caused it."

"No, David, the war caused it; she recorded it."

He watched her walk back across the room and then looked down into the case that held the marine exhibit. How stupid it was . . . all those dried-up sea horses and starfish, dusty and crumbling, deader than the Roman battle axe. In his museum there would be no natural history; no stuffed birds, dried lizards, dead fish, pinned butterflies, pickled fetuses, animals worked over by the taxidermist. None of the death that pretends to imitate life.

Brock's coat. Bullets and buttons and cannon-balls. The cannons themselves, if he could find them. And endless scarlet uniforms, empty, no dummies propping them up. Maps, autographs, commissions signed by famous generals. He would like to have a special section given over entirely to the art of oratory, though he couldn't decide quite how to manage it – copies of great speeches given by men approaching battle.

His wife called him again, this time to a case which purported to hold the first poem written in Canada . . . the first of a never-ending series of responses to Niagara Falls.

He couldn't imagine why anyone would want to save this anonymous, none too enlightening, piece of verse. It told him absolutely nothing.

His wife, however, was looking at the fragment with great intensity ... as though she could see the pen, the ink, the expression of a human being bothered by a waterfall that had made its home inside the brain.

"I am wondering," she said, almost to herself, "if it is this that Patrick wants from the whirlpool. Perhaps he wants to carry some of it away with him in words."

From deep inside the fixed idea of the poet, Fleda looked out at her husband. David hadn't heard her. He was trying to solve the puzzle of Brock's hat.

She sighed and sunk a little deeper into her thoughts of Patrick, allowing them to cushion her now, to protect her from the sordid, the ordinary, the real.

⌒

14 August 1889

𝒯 This is how it is now. There are days when he does watch me and days when he doesn't. I am looking for a pattern. Last week I thought I had it; I thought it was every second afternoon. But this week he hasn't appeared for three days running . . . except in the evenings when David is here. But then it's as if he is someone else. This should not be, but is a disappointment to me.

At times today I have been sure that I felt him moving through the woods towards me, towards the tent. But he doesn't arrive. Strange how I search the woods for him, look down the bank towards the whirlpool.

He is out there somewhere, hidden. Now, without even a glimpse, without even the faintest rustle of branches, I can feel his scrutiny.

I've even begun to dress for him. I have a new skirt – pale blue silk with white braid. David says that it's ridiculous that I should want to wear it here in the woods. How I love it, though, and the way the sun touches it. Nothing is ever military enough for David or illusive enough for Patrick.

How do I know this? I know absolutely nothing really.

It seems he has a wife in Ottawa and some sort of government employment. All of this is beyond the powers of my imagination.

I want him to come out of the forest; to speak to me and I want him to continue to watch me.

Sometimes I want him to touch me.

Is this the responsibility of the whirlpool? Has it become a whirlwind, scraping the earth with the back of its hand until we are all caught in it?

No, you have to enter the whirlpool by choice. You have to walk towards it and step into it. Or you have to be pushed.

It's only the ocean's maelstrom that you slip into by chance, moving in a straight line from this to that.

Perhaps I've always waited for the demon lover to leave the maelstrom and enter my house, through some window while I slept on . . . innocent and unaware.

One moment you are dreaming, the next terrifyingly awake, on board a ghost ship bound for God knows where . . . away from home.

Away from home . . . it is the open sea, the damp, a storm approaching and the inevitable shipwreck.

Would it not also be true that at this moment of disaster you would know exactly who you were? Not necessarily who you had been, but who you were right then?

Interesting that the demon attacks only architecture. In the woods it is knights, dragons, and ladies who are eventually set free.

Perhaps you have to be lodged in order to be dislodged.

> *"Savage I was sitting in my house*
> *late, lone*
> *Dreary, weary with the long day's work*
> *Head of me, heart of me, stupid as stone."*
>   *R.B.   The Householder*

Dislodge: to remove, turn out from position.
Perhaps the knowledge comes at the moment of departure.

Ω

*"The whirlpool is not only down there," Patrick moved his head towards the bank, "it's also up here." He waved his other hand vaguely somewhere above his head. "I've been to the observatory in Ottawa and I've seen it. Now the whole idea makes me dizzy, interferes with my sense of gravity."

Fleda looked at him and waited for him to continue. She could hear the rapids in the silence. They were louder today; something to do with wind and a low covering of clouds.

"You see," he said, "there are stars in a spiral pattern up there ... nebulae ... the question is ... are they moving?"

"Probably," said Fleda. "They couldn't just be standing still."

"Why not," he wanted to know, "why couldn't they just be standing still?"

"Because nothing does, nothing ever, ever does."

"There is air around me all the time," Patrick continued, "and gravity ... it's like being continually immersed."

Fleda was becoming uncomfortable. They had never spoken together like this. Still she moved forward.

"You move through it, though," she said. "You come here and you go away. It doesn't stop you."

"One pulls me down and the other slows me down."

"You want to live weightless ..."

177

"Yes, one wants to live weightless, but just can't. Everything moves around but gravity pulls you down and the air sticks to the body like a shroud."

Fleda tried to imagine the air as some other kind of substance, heavier. It would be like water, then, like trying to walk through water. But air wasn't like that ... not for her.

"But for you, it wouldn't be like that," he said, reading her thoughts.

Fleda was aware of fear hovering somewhere close to her consciousness. But she couldn't place it, couldn't give it an exact location. They hadn't walked farther than forty yards away from the tent, where David was writing. But the forest was thick here, seemed to isolate them somehow, close them in together in an accidental intimacy. Except in her imagination, she had never talked to Patrick like this before. She began to speak quickly, the first things that came into her mind.

"About gravity," she said, "the oddest thing happened last winter."

Patrick backed up a step.

"David and I had been to a party at Prospect House. A sort of late New Year's. It was very stormy, windy ... I almost froze going down there in the cutter. Anyway, when we left, around one a.m., when we left and went outside, we looked at the Suspension Bridge in the wind. It was actually heaving, moving up and down in the wind like a whip. Just as I was about to point this out to David, it snapped ... broke in two and fell into the gorge."

"You *saw* that?"

"Yes, and I thought, I have been back and forth on that bridge a hundred times. David not so often – he doesn't like to go over there. I enjoyed crossing it, just to look down at the rapids. And suddenly ... the connection is broken, forever. But then," she added, laughing, "David said that the connection should be broken ... with the Americans, I mean."

Patrick's emotions were suddenly and inexplicably meshing with this arbitrary topic. Involuntarily, he moved closer and reached towards the woman's sleeve with his open palm. A gesture which, when he interrupted it, looked like one of caution. "But, Fleda," he said, "think! That first bridge, the one you crossed over and over, that bridge is *gone*. It won't ever come back."

"In a way, it was like a broken habit," Fleda remarked. "I could have crossed it blindfolded, I knew it that well. And one storm and it's gone! I guess it surprised me to discover that something can disappear like that so irrevocably from your life."

"Things can and do." Patrick leaned casually against a tree, pretending to be relaxed. "You let yourself get too close to the bridge," he said. "You couldn't see it any more. That's what happened. You didn't know it was dangerous ... it took a violent storm to show you that it was weak. Weak and dangerous. You had to see it in completely altered circumstances. It had to be flapping in a shrieking wind before you could see it as it really was. Weak and dangerous."

"Yes, but if I had looked that carefully ... if I had known ... I never would have crossed at all. I never would have seen the rapids from above."

"Precisely ... you allowed yourself to get too close to the bridge and then you couldn't see it properly. You trusted it, when, in fact, it was completely untrustworthy."

They were deep in the woods though not at all far from the tent.

They began to gather the kindling they had gone there to collect. A short shower earlier in the day had left the wood in the open areas drenched. In here, though, there was such a mesh of overhead green that the rain had been unable to break through and the twigs which lay on the ground were completely dry.

"You have gotten close to the whirlpool," Fleda said suddenly, after breaking a long stick in two with her foot. "I've seen you. You have looked right at it from the very edge of the shore."

"I haven't," said Patrick, "been anywhere near its centre. That I can only see from a distance . . . or through the glasses, which is merely an illusion. What do you think exists at the centre?" Once again Patrick was unsure if it was the whirlpool or the woman he was talking of.

As if she had travelled at great speeds over an endless space, Fleda felt herself for the first time close to Patrick. As if he had touched her on the shoulder or placed his hand, momentarily, on her hair. She thought she might be able to ask him now, about his approach . . . and about his avoidance.

"But, you haven't allowed me . . . you would never allow me . . ." she began.

"No, I haven't, have I," said Patrick, interrupting her.

"I would try to talk to you . . . and you would stop me . . . I can't even say how . . . but you would do it and I would be stopped."

"I was afraid."

"Why were you afraid?"

"It has to do with untrustworthy connections."

"I am untrustworthy, then, even to speak to?"

"I spoke . . ."

"Not really . . . you would want me to talk and then silence me."

"Yes," he admitted.

It began to rain again, this time an even, steady curtain of water. They were protected in the thicket of green – shut in together, a closeness concocted by nature. Fleda searched her mind for something else to say. She wanted to keep Patrick there, in the green cocoon, with the rain eliminating the rest of the world. She wanted him to speak and come nearer.

"And if you had swum the whirlpool already, you wouldn't be afraid?"

"Not of the whirlpool."

Fleda was silent. She looked upward at the top branches, wondering when the rain would break through, how long they would be protected. She thought about the fear, how he felt it too; whether, when he described it, it was his fear or hers he was referring to. If it belonged to both of them it would be like a third person, then, always with them, so that they would never be close or alone together.

"I would have hoped . . ." she said to Patrick, aware that she might never have another chance. "I would have hoped that we might have been able to get close to each other . . . that we might have been friends."

They stood and looked at each other, each with their arms full of sticks for some future fire. A blanket of rain all over the forest and this one clearing a bubble of open air. Then the rain broke through and the fear in Patrick snapped into focus.

He dropped his bundle of kindling on the ground and moved swiftly towards Fleda. Grabbing her shoulders he thrust his face into hers, so close she could feel the hot breath of his words on her face.

"Learn this," he hissed, "I don't *want* to be this close to you. Not now, not ever. Look what happens . . . when we're this close we can't see each other at all . . . not even each other's eyes. This close, you're a blur . . . and I'm nothing . . . completely nothing . . . nothing but a voice. You can't see me. My voice is so close it could be inside your own head. I don't *want* to be this close, Fleda. I want the distance."

She shook him off and moved back several feet, clutching her own bundle of wood to her heart, frightened and hurt. Rain all over her face.

"You DO!" She turned on him, her voice rising. "You DO! I've seen you . . . I KNOW how you are thinking. I know," she finally blurted out, "that you have been watching me

... wanting something. Why else would you watch me like that? You WANT to be close to me!"

Patrick began to shake. He felt that his privacy, his self, had been completely invaded. He was like a walled village that had been sacked and burned, just when it was feeling most secure, when it was full of provisions and all the people and livestock were safe behind the drawbridge. How *dare* she? he thought as if she, not he, had been the voyeur.

"You're wrong," he said coldly. "I've never watched you."

"But Patrick," she said, her voice softer now, "it's all right. I don't mind. I'm glad that you watched me." She saw herself, momentarily, through his eyes ... a legend in a forest.

He was furious. It was as if this ordinary woman, this housewife, had turned his brain inside out so that she could examine it scientifically. His fantasy became a smear on a glass under a lens in a laboratory.

"I don't know what you are talking about," he said, trying to control his trembling voice, "but whatever it is, I think we should stop discussing it."

Fleda was silent, shocked. She stared hard at his face.

Patrick did not look at her, would never look at her again. She was not supposed to be aware of the focus of the lens he had fixed on her. She was never meant to answer his attentions. She had now pulled his fantasy into the mundane architecture of fact.

He left her there, alone in the woods, and made his way, angrily, through the storm, back to his uncle's farm.

*

Very rarely, but now and then, a perfect corpse came down the river to the whirlpool. With all the unreliability of chance it slid around murderous rocks and avoided currents destined for sharp branches. As if it knew the river well and could navigate its courses.

And sometimes, the coolness of the water preserved rather than decayed these bodies, adding a shine to skin bleached white as marble.

These few luminous corpses were like pale messages to Maud. They spoke of beings at home in water, content with the voyages it took them on. They spoke of ancient rivers and the sea inside the womb. Maud buried them unhappily, convinced the earth was foreign to them, an unsuitable pallet for the last long slumber.

During the three days she kept them in the stable there was little need of ice; the flesh was firm, the features exact. They looked, often, as if they might speak, softly, of the smooth ride in the river or the slow dance of limbs in water. Anyone might have recognized their faces, their hands, a scar left from childhood on a knee.

But nearly always they went to the graveyard unclaimed, unidentified. As if the whole process, the drowning, the intricate voyage over rapids, the circular swim in the whirlpool, had been for Maud's benefit alone.

So that very rarely, but now and then, she might have something perfect, undamaged, beautiful to describe in her little leather book.

ℐ

Patrick was remembering evenings in Ottawa – the recollection so intense he could practically feel the heat from the fireplace reach his knees. And then the cold. His eyes fixed on the black and white of the evening paper. Facts. His mind numb, empty of poetry.

The dull, turgid repetition of everything reproduced in the click of his wife's knitting needles. He realized, now, that he had not stopped, ever, to ask what it was she was making. He had no idea whether she was working on a series of items or if the knitting was part of some unfathomable lengthy project to which there might never be an end. He tried to remember the colour of the wool but was denied any sort of mental picture. His mind returned to the sound of knitting needles, sliding against each other, and his wife's sighs as she bent forward in her chair to lift another ball of wool from the basket at her feet.

In the daytime it had been the scratch, scratch of his own pen that had irritated him, sometimes to the point of frenzy. Recording numbers, keeping records of irrelevant transactions. The verticals of lists and columns, so unnatural to him when his mind sought the free sweep of a line of verse. He was angered, finally, even by the shape of the copy book, a desk shape, a volume designed for facts. Nothing for the hand, the mind, or the soul to hold.

Now his image of Fleda had been violated, soiled by everything he had tried to escape from. She became the smudge of the news on his fingers, the ink from his employment on his hands, the ugly red brick of his small house.

Still, there was a swimmer in his mind and that swimmer would descend the bank without the woman, alone. Then he could study the current, which, because of the way it moved, he believed could never stun him the way the immobility of facts did.

Early afternoon and he was standing by the white picket fence on Main Street with the intention of gaining access to the McDougal's rooms when they were not there. Some story about retrieving the little book he had left with the major, or perhaps something about an errand. He needed to verify the fact of the woman as she seemed now – ordinary, an accumulator of property, a keeper of houses. A configuration of objects she had organized, the position of her books on a shelf, how her jewellery was arranged in a satin box would disclose this wordly side of her. Then he would be through with her.

The child, playing alone in the east corner of the garden spotted Patrick at once. Running over to him, shouting "Man, man, man," he attached himself firmly to the sleeve of his jacket by reaching one small arm between two of the upright boards of the fence.

"Forest," he greeted Patrick, happily.

"Hullo," said Patrick, rather sharply, trying to disengage the child's hand.

"Hotel," said the child, clutching Patrick's sleeve more tightly.

"Yes, I *am* looking at the hotel," admitted Patrick in a tone that suggested a certain amount of disgust.

"Looking," the boy repeated.

"I am looking at the hotel," Patrick continued, almost

sarcastically, "because I am hoping to make some discoveries."

"Hoping," said the child.

Gerunds, thought Patrick, those verbal nouns. Today is a day of gerunds, clearly. *Looking, discovering, discarding, denying.* He looked at the child who appeared to be anxiously awaiting another sentence.

"Well," ventured Patrick, "here we are talking."

"Talking," said the child.

"Perhaps I'll start walking." Patrick paced a few steps back and forth in front of the boy.

"Walking."

"Now I'm stalking," said Patrick, beginning to creep around in a circle.

"Stalk-ing."

"All this looking at the hotel," said Patrick, starting to laugh, "is simply gawking."

"Gawking," said the boy, with a giggle.

"If anyone heard us talking, they'd think we were utterly shocking." Patrick laughed out loud.

The boy laughed too. "Shock-*king*," he yelled merrily.

"If I were standing in front of this gate and you wanted to get out – " Patrick laughed again – "then I'd be blocking."

The child rocked back and forth in glee. "Blocking," he gasped.

Patrick rapped the side of the fence three times and guffawed. "Knocking," he announced, doubling over with mirth.

The laughter had taken hold of them both by now, shaking their rib-cages and rattling their windpipes. The child, holding his stomach, rolled around on the soft grass. Patrick, tears cascading down his cheeks, clutched the gatepost for support. "Listen," he began. "Listen to us. . . ." Then, another paroxysm silenced him. He tried again. "Now," he managed to sputter, "now we are squawking! You, you especially." Patrick pointed to the boy. "You are squawking."

"You are squaw-*king*," rejoined the boy.

"No, that's not what I said. I said that *you* are squawking." The boy stopped laughing. Patrick pointed to himself and said the word "I." Then he pointed at the boy and said the word "you."

The boy pointed at Patrick and said the word "I." Then he pointed at himself and said the word "you."

Patrick, quite serious now, tears drying on his lashes, took hold of the boy's hand from the other side of the fence. Scrambling his perceptions in order to reach the child, he pointed to the centre of the boy's blue jacket and said, very slowly, the word "I." Then he pointed to his own breastbone and said the word "you."

"You," said the child, stroking Patrick's sleeve.

"Yes, yes," said Patrick, sighing. He looked over his shoulder at the hotel. Self and other. That's the way it always was. To merge was impossible except for short periods of time. Impossible and undesirable. He imagined the woman, aware of his watching, possibly even performing. The idea filled him with horror.

He gently removed the child's little hand from his jacket. "Now I am going."

"Now you are going," said the child.

"Good, yes, correct." Patrick stepped away from the fence, glancing at the windows of the hotel as he did so. Then he strolled away on the board sidewalk, descending the hill on foot rather than taking the trolley.

The boy watched the man become smaller and smaller, and then watched the hill move up like a wall behind him. First there was the whole man, then just a torso, then his head, and then he was gone.

𝒥

Since childhood Patrick had had recurring dreams about his uncle's farmhouse. The very magnitude of it had seized his imagination.

Growing up in the cramped quarters of his father's simple lodgings, he was unused to architectural structures whose corners, windows, staircases, and basements could not be taken in in a single phrase of thought. His uncle's house, to him, was a series of paragraphs, each one containing a subject entirely separate from the last.

The driveshed, although it functioned as one of the main entrances to the house, was a dark and disconnected world where the giant wheels of wagons were barely discernible in the gloom. The place reeked of damp; of black soil and mildewed burlap. It was the location of iron and leather and tin, harnesses, discarded washtubs, broken ploughs. It was where all cutting instruments were stored, teeth and blades, jagged edges of saws, soft shine of a sharpened axe. The boards, which extended around the shed's perimeter, and which were used for walking purposes, were worn smooth by generations of men's boots. The flash of a woman's skirt through these premises was a shock to the environment – the way surroundings seem, sometimes, to respond to the sudden appearance of a trapped bird, which can be terrifying in the stillness of an undisturbed room.

Latch lifted and door pushed away from this spot, one entered another geography – that of the kitchen. Smells, colours, temperature, textures, underwent an abrupt change and, for Patrick the child, a change not quite so easy to undergo. It seemed to him that he carried the after-image of the driveshed's unspecified menace with him into the warmth and activity of the kitchen, so that the loaf of bread rising on the counter, the plants unfurling on the windowsill, were charged with an almost imperceptible, ominous growth that frightened him, as did the voluminous cook, incessantly stirring by the stove.

This was a cumulative effect, and each room led to another without the transitional stage of a hall, though it too, had it existed, might have been pulled into the process. From the kitchen one passed directly into the dining room, and into this cool, still, formal space, Patrick carried the mood of earth and blades and machinery from the shed and the silent blind growth of the kitchen. Here, he could see his face change in a variety of polished surfaces: silver and mahogany, the glass doors of the china cabinet. Reflections and silence and a complete absence of dust. Patrick, knowing he was carrying by this time something of both the other rooms with him, began to believe he had a face for each. His dark expression, glowing in mahogany, was his driveshed self, the face that shone back at him from silver was one that he had acquired from the photosynthetic light of the kitchen, and in the cool transparency of glass where he could place his features over the objects behind it, a visage was given to him as a result of exposure to the dining room itself.

And so it continued, through the stuffed and billowing forms in the parlour, to the horizontals of the bedrooms with their large and frightening mirrors in which, Patrick believed, anything at all might appear. Any one of the ground-floor rooms could be entered into from the outside, but Patrick chose, as a form of thrilling self-torture, to follow the emotionally charged route of rooms that led to rooms that led to rooms, as if he were an explorer on the verge of a great discovery.

In his dreams, despite the fact that they were recurring, the discovery always came as a surprise. At the end of the parlour, in the position normally occupied by a large window, Patrick would find a door. His feeling of surprise would soon be replaced by one of intense curiosity and he would pull it open to be confronted with a narrow staircase which led, as might be expected, to rooms that led to rooms that led to rooms – a replica, in fact, of the ground floor of the house, except that the contents would be entirely scrambled. In this space, the dining room with its cold, blue walls and perfectly regular flooring, was filled with wheels and teeth and blades and smelled of damp, rotting burlap. The harsh, golden light of the kitchen, on the other hand, would expose undulating sinks and counters, soft tables and doughboards resembling the overstuffed furniture of the parlour. The parlour had become as smooth and untouched as ice; its surfaces reflecting not its own contents at all but those of rooms Patrick had never even imagined until that moment.

He would awaken, always, with blood pounding in his head and an intense fear that all the objects in the room where he slept would suddenly be unfamiliar and out of context.

As he grew older, the dream visited him less and less until, as he entered his twenties, it happened only once every two or three years. The fear that accompanied the dream subsided as well. Between occurrences of the nightmare there were long periods during which he forgot about it altogether.

But now, in his early thirties, walking through the rooms of his uncle's house, carrying the anger towards the woman with him in his mind, he abruptly remembered it and, for the first time, understood its meaning, its message. Keep the sequence of fear, of quest, of desire in logical order – compartmentalized and exact. Try not to bring one with you into the other. Do not confuse fear with desire, desire with quest, quest with fear. Otherwise the world scrambles, becomes unidentifiable, loses its recognizable context.

A simple shift of objects, events, emotions, from their rightful place brings chaos. And the world you live in enters nightmare.

He had dislocated and mixed categories, had confused the woman with the whirlpool, had believed, in some crazy way, that she *was* the landscape that she walked around in every day. It was landscape that he wanted and needed, uncomplicated setting, its ability to function and endure in a pure, solitary state. He could enter it and depart from it without altering one drop of water, a single leaf on a tree. The forest, the whirlpool, could touch him and change him and remain as strong and relentless as they ever were before.

There would be no more confusion. He was through with the woman. From now on, whenever he visited Whirlpool Heights, and he knew he would visit often, it would be the landscape he was courting.

⁊

As far as her husband was concerned nothing had changed. But for Fleda, who had been training herself to look for nuances, everything had. Something about the way Patrick's eyes moved told her that, even though he behaved with utter courtesy towards her when he visited, there would be no turning back from their confrontation in the forest. He was gone. Or perhaps the part of her that he had secretly examined had been dismissed by him, simply eliminated by a new brand of selective amnesia. Once, just days ago, he had still looked at her. But not now.

She felt like an abandoned house. He was closing doors, drawing curtains, nailing windows shut. The dream, the image he had created was being boarded up, condemned, and its demolition had already begun.

His eyes travelling from place to place when she was there, never stopping, avoiding focus. It was as if he were watching a frantic insect, trapped in the tent, moving, moving, never coming to rest. Outside, they followed the flight of birds, the passing of clouds, the unpredictable behaviour of the wind in the trees. At night he gazed at fire, but uncontemplatively ... he actually scrutinized it, mirroring its erratic movements with his new, restless eyes.

Her first reaction was anger. How could he disappear, go from her like this? She had *felt* his attention. They had talked once, maybe twice ... never really touched, but she had known about the focus of his mind. And now this was gone; the complex symbolism that had described the meaning behind the meaning. This absence was something taken from her ... leaving her flat and empty, and the life she had lived before became impossible to re-enter.

Fleda's second reaction was pain; a sense of loss so brutal it stunned and confused her. How could she possibly lose something she had never had? No matter. This was foreign matter clogged in her throat, choking her, but not quite. It would neither completely leave her nor completely suffocate her. Not a terminal but a chronic disease.

And then, to make his act of treason, of denial, complete and sure, Patrick removed her last hope. He did not stay away. If he had, she might have been able to move these tiny particles of experience into her memory, place them in a special chamber and make them beautiful. As it was, he was now, more than ever, present in their lives; unravelling what he had woven. She knew, and she suspected he knew, that his extended presence after this change would continuously diminish her in his own memory, possibly even in hers. She would shrink and shrink, years would move out from her like an unblemished highway, until she would become a detail lost in the greater whole. Eventually, she might disappear altogether.

This was too much for her to bear. She would not be discarded, disposed of like this. She had felt his attention around her, even when he wasn't there. She had felt herself a part of his quest, his desire to break free, to attempt the whirlpool. Part of the creation of poetry.

As if to fill his former ambiguous silence – the space that Fleda knew she had occupied – with evidence of the ordinary, he began to talk. He talked and talked ... about suspension bridges, about the St. David's buried gorge, about the war, about Indians, about Confederation. He talked about the Fenian Raids, the spiral nebulae, Walt Whitman and Butler's

Rangers. He talked about the Falls, how they were eating their way up the Niagara River. A terrifying image, he announced . . . sublime! They might, in time, devour the whole borderline. David had laughed then, delighted by the young man's wit, his cleverness.

In a subtle shift of alliance, he entered David's territory, cunningly, as if he had been there all along. Fleda was isolated, other, driven to remote corners of the acre, taking long, desperate walks along the bank overlooking the whirlpool, while they talked and talked, excluding her.

No day was safe from him. Once, Fleda returned in the late afternoon to the sound of hammers bouncing from tree to tree. Three carpenters had just begun work on the carriage house which was to be situated just beyond the main building. Patrick and David had opened a bottle of wine in celebration, were toasting the building, the invisible house, each other. Patrick was standing in front of David.

"Next year I'll come back and you will have built it, a house, right here, where once there was nothing at all."

Nothing at all, thought Fleda, unobserved, though standing near them in the forest. *Nothing, nothing at all*.

She would send him away, she decided. She would not let his betrayal slide away without comment. She would make an articulate summary of what she felt, what she *knew* had happened. She would bring it to his attention, *his attention*, and then she would send him away.

The anger awakened her in the middle of the night, pounding in her ears. And the pain stayed, lodged in her throat, a piece of glass, a rusty tin can, a bundle of burdock.

Corners were being introduced into her geography, accompanied by enthusiastic comments from the men. The building was a woman. "She looks good, don't you think? Shouldn't she have a back door too? She'll be big enough for two good-sized carriages." Pushing back their hats, they stood looking upwards at timber, at straight lines and corners, at the artificiality of geometric order. Fleda held on to the tent, even though she began to feel it was becoming extinct. A memory, a monument to another fading time.

In the end she did nothing at all. She let him go and she let him stay. She did not speak her pain, her anger. She began to write small notes to herself, tiny, etched, painful lines on torn paper. These she hid in her long sleeves or in her corset. She recorded her dreams; ones where he was conclusively absent or conclusively present, ones where he appeared as a bird or a fish. She leafed, for the first time, through his book, vaguely noting a word here or there and letting no word touch her.

She let him go. The man who visited had nothing to do with the other, the one in her dreams, the absent one. She was able, within days, to speak pleasantly to the man who visited, while mourning steadily for the one who had, as she perceived it now, completely abandoned her. This visitor was David's friend, a man she could talk with but one she was closed to.

The other in the dream house in her mind.

I

19 August 1889

I have read his poems over and over. There are no people in them, no emotion. Just acres of forest, acres of rock and unrelenting winter. I read them coldly, as if I were the grey, uncaring sky which covers the bleak landscape he speaks about. There is nothing there for me.

"A common grayness silvers everything."

He tells David he will be returning soon to Ottawa. I tell a humorous story concerning David's departure for the camp at Niagara when he was left in charge there three summers ago. He was obsessed by his spurs, though I'm certain they never once came close to the delicate flesh of his sainted horse. I, of course, packed his trunk . . . starched shirts, underwear, boots, collars, breeches, etc., and the spurs. "Are you sure they are in there?" he would constantly ask me. "Positive, certain, absolutely without a doubt!" I would assure him, over and over.

Then the second I left the room he would throw everything out of the trunk in a frantic and panic-stricken search for the spurs which were, of course, there. I would repack the trunk and three days later we would reenact the entire ritual.

I finally decided that he either didn't want to go to the camp at all or he didn't want to take his spurs with him. When I packed the trunk for the third and final time, I purposely hid the spurs in a bureau drawer, handing them over only when he was making his final exit out of the front door.

As I tell this story Patrick laughs quietly. David scowls into the fire. But I know, nonetheless, that he is pleased that the anecdote I am relating is centred around him.

Now I have come to believe that the trunk should be unpacked before the journey, rather than after ... that its contents should be taken out and scattered to the winds.

> "Shop was shop only; household stuff?
> What did he want with comforts there?
> Walls, ceiling, floor, stay blank and rough
> So goods on sale show rich and rare
> Sell and send home, *be shop's affair.*"
> R.B. *Shop*

20 August 1889

I don't believe that Patrick is going to swim the whirlpool, though I will not ask him.

All he speaks of now is the war, and when he is speaking he is not talking to me.

David thoroughly enjoys this. They have both decided that war is an abstract theory meaning something else entirely.

Patrick says that he totally rejects the concept of an audience when it comes to battle ... that participation is all.

David reminds him over and over that the future is the audience and that the future is the present now ... so, he wonders, where is the audience?

Patrick says that it is in the United States.

Then they both laugh a lot.

Still, Patrick sometimes goes down to scrutinize the whirlpool. I've been watching and I've seen him.

Once when they were talking I read some of the last verses of R.B.'s "Amphibian" aloud to them both, slowly and with much expression:

XI

"But sometimes when the weather
Is blue and warm waves tempt
To free one's life from tether
And try a life exempt

XII

From worldly noise and dust
In the sphere which overbrims
With passion and thought – why just
Unable to fly, one swims

XIV

Emancipate through passion
And thought, with sea for sky
We substitute, in a fashion
For heaven – poetry."

II

Maud collapsed on the chaise lounge in the sunroom. She was exhausted, completely exhausted, by the humidity. In the garden her zinnias drooped, unable to flounce their colour in this heavy air. Only yesterday the wind that had formerly moved the atmosphere around, had abruptly stopped. Now Maud had the feeling that she was breathing the same air over and over, that it would never change, never go anywhere else. The thought oppressed her.

She had sent the child off with the housekeeper, unable to cope with another moment in his presence. Unable to listen any more to what he had to say, for now there was something new. He had begun to fill up the adults' silences with a verbal description of their actions, as senselessly as Maud's former naming of objects in her external environment. Back when she still wanted him to talk. Very soon, she decided, the child would reduce them all, not only to silence, but to paralysis as well.

Now you are climbing the stairs, he would say, struggling along after her. Now you have come to the top, now you are walking down the hall. Now you can't remember what you came up here for. Now you are going into the parlour. Now you are picking up the mail from the tray. Now you are going back to the hall. Now you are walking back into the sunroom. Now you are in the sunroom.

"You must stop this senseless behaviour," she would shout at him, "there's no reason for it!"

"You must stop this senseless behaviour," he would shout back, "there's no reason for it!"

"Now you are looking straight at the boy," he would continue, "and you are very angry at him."

There were momentary interruptions in all this. The child had learned that language could be moulded into requests. But he hadn't yet made use of the pronouns "I" or "me," always referred to himself as "the boy." "The boy is hungry, the boy is tired, the boy wants to go out into the garden."

"What is your name?" Maud once asked him in desperation.

He had looked around behind him, as if to assure himself no one else was being addressed, then, "What is your name?" he had replied.

She was astonished by the extent of his vocabulary; even in a normal child of his age it would have been remarkable. But for one who had held onto silence for years, the variety of words was overwhelming. As though he had been storing verbal symbols in a special cerebral enclosure until it became so full it simply had to burst. He had drawn the world that circled him inwards, had hoarded snippets of discourse, and then all of this tumbled out of his mouth like a mountain waterfall after the ice on the heights has melted.

His talk about the man persisted. Maud was beginning to believe that the child might be referring to another side of himself, as recently he had combined the words "man" and "mine." He would become agitated at these times, running from window to window, looking up and down Main Street, whispering the words "man" and "mine" over and over, or occasionally shouting them at Maud as if he expected her to do something, to perform some kind of anticipated miracle.

Maud knew the heavy air would eventually break . . . break into the true weather of this country, the safe cold when the river appeared to stop. Then there would be a pause, a time for ordinary funerals, when her little notebook could be stored in a dark drawer and the hall cupboard door closed.

Outside, a few of the maple's leaves rustled unexpectedly and then were still. Through the open window Maud heard the child talking to a bird.

"Now you are going to fly away," he said.

⁂

Order attacked the child as suddenly, as unpredictably as any other form of disease, and he began to sort, to classify.

Maud was surprised one morning to find her haphazardly arranged dresser drawers immaculate; gloves placed together in one location, stockings in another. The housekeeper could not have done this. Maud kept her own room, had always done so.

At first she could not imagine what had happened, and tried to remember whether she, herself, in a distracted, preoccupied way, had actually performed the task while thinking about something else. She had lost objects in this manner, moving them unconsciously around the house while her mind arranged an important funeral, but never in her experience had she organized drawers ... consciously or otherwise.

Then she guessed it. The child; the child had done this, slipping through the house like a shadow. Vaguely pleased with this new facet of his behaviour, she decided to let it rest. No harm done, no harm.

She closed the window in her room as she did each morning after a night filled with the perils of vapours, and walked through the doorway down the hall to the sunroom, the light of which burst easily over her as she reached her desk.

Settling in, she opened the drawer to remove the accounts book. There, also, order surprised her. Seven lead pencils were arranged according to size in descending scale at the front. Beside them, two erasers, their pink tips and bottoms not a fraction out of line. Adjacent to these lay her gum-backed labels in a pile so regular it resembled a tiny block of wood painted red and white. Her several notebooks were piled, one on top of the other, at the rear of the drawer, like a miniature ziggurat, beginning with the largest account book at the bottom and finishing with the smallest (her collection of drowned individuals) at the top. Now she was beginning to become perplexed. An isolated incident was one thing, but what else had he been into besides drawers?

She was staring into the many cubbyholes directly above the surface of the desk when she realized that the familiar irregularity of the papers she stashed there had also changed. All the envelopes (mostly containing IOU's) had been filed, again according to size, with the smaller ones occupying smaller spaces, the larger, larger spaces and the unclassifiable nowhere to be seen. The child had clearly taken it upon himself to dispose of these irregularities. If they couldn't be sorted, then they shouldn't exist.

Maud looked around the room and noted, as she now feared, that its profusion of bric-a-brac was undeniably altered. Objects had been grouped together, classified somehow, though it was difficult for Maud to determine the criteria for these new configurations. Her domestic geography had been tampered with, her home had become a puzzle. The size classification that the child had so neatly applied to the desk was not in evidence anywhere else in the room. Instead, there were these innumerable clusters of small connected objects, some that had been in the room previously, some that had been brought from other rooms to complete a bizarre design determined by the child.

The mantel, she discovered, was covered with cutting, shining things: her letter opener, a pen-knife, three needles from her sewing basket, scissors, a razor blade, which had somehow remained in the house since Charles' death, and a piece of broken glass. A cherry sidetable, which normally held Charles' photo, appeared to be empty. But as Maud looked again, it revealed itself to be covered with various forms of detritus: a dust ball, lint from a cotton pocket, a small amount of sand apparently from the driveway, and, most strange, a dirty, soot-filled spider web, found in some corner, no doubt, that she was unaware of, or perhaps from the workshops downstairs. There were ashes, too, probably from the cook stove in the kitchen.

The photograph of Charles? She found it, after searching for some time, situated under the curving arm of the sofa, along with others of her parents, his parents, herself. These were combined with a variety of other flat human images; a paper doll, a steel engraving from *Ladies' Home Journal*, and a framed lithograph, from the parlour, of a little girl staring out to sea.

On the windowsill, the presence of a clear paperweight, the magnifying glass her mother-in-law had used to read, her father-in-law's spectacles, and a pressed glass goblet confounded Maud until she realized that what they had in common was transparency and an innate ability to shatter.

She wondered which had come to the child first: the fairly simple method of classification according to size, or the more complex method of classification by physical property. There were groups of objects, moreover, whose common denominator she couldn't, for the life of her, identify: the thimble, pearl necklace, and spoon, for instance, or the playing card, chestnut, and emery board.

Maud moved around the room in a bemused manner, taking stock of the situation. The appearance of objects from further rooms caused her to suppose that the whole house had been disturbed as much as it might have been had vandals ransacked it during the night. It would be weeks before her own concept of order was restored. Still, she could not yet become angry. Every time she tried, her curiosity got in the way. These strange little assemblings might be the key to the child's mind; a garden she'd been denied access to for years. In her heart, she felt like letting him continue. Rearrange it, she would say, it might be better.

On the bookshelf, in front of *Great Expectations* and *Little Dorrit*, was a collection of tickets of various sizes ... just that, no more; a colourful collection of tickets. Nothing complex here. These came from the ferry boat, or the streetcar, or the opera house ... a few from the Terrapin Tower or other amusements near the Falls. One was from a horse race. Maud shuffled them in her fingers, pondering their significance in the child's mind.

It came to her slowly, the origin of these tickets, very slowly at first. Then, the knowledge exploding in her head like fireworks, she turned and ran from the room, down the long hall. The child, she suddenly knew, had invaded her cupboard, her museum.

∬

S This morning being Sunday, and none of them at church, they were sitting on three camp stools near the bank. Patrick had arrived early, his trousers soaked with the dew that had covered the orchards he had to cross on his route from the farm to the Heights. He had helped himself to the coffee that bubbled over the fire and had accepted an offer of bacon and eggs. He and David discussed and then rejected the idea of church, looking as pleased as schoolboys taking a day off.

All of this is so innocent, Fleda thought to herself angrily. The men had a secret pact. They knew what they should do and they knew how to be gleefully guilty when they weren't doing it. Never a thought that desire and duty could possibly mesh. Never a thought that the deepest desires were a duty in themselves. Somehow she felt that the men would either snicker or turn away in horror from her intensest wishes, even though they had some, not unlike hers, locked away in some corner of their heads – in a place where she couldn't get at them, and they couldn't either.

She began to hum hymns, quietly, and then with increasing volume, when she realized that neither man was paying any attention. They were discussing the war.

"Did I ever show you the garden in Queenston where Brock paused to draw his breath, just before he scaled the

Heights?" David was asking. "Just imagine him there, alive one minute in a *flower garden*, and the next hour completely dead."

Fleda decided to add words to the tune she was humming:

Rescue the perishing, care for the dying.
Snatch them in pity from sin and the grave

"Why did he do it, do you think?" Patrick opened his hands earnestly. "Was it for the sake of a magnificent death? He must have known. Wouldn't he have known?"

"You have to remember," David continued didactically, "that Brock would have had Nelson as a model and General Wolfe. These men were happy to use their bodies as targets."

"Targets?"

"Um-hmm, a wonderful thing to do. After all, to aim at the leader distracts the enemy, if only briefly."

"*Soldiers of Christ arise, and put your armour on*," Fleda sang. And then:

Leave no unguarded place
No weakness of the soul
Take every virtue, every grace
And fortify the whole

As a child she had memorized practically the whole Canadian Hymnal, it being the closest thing to poetry that graced the shelves of her father's house. She remembered the shape of the book ... its cover was oddly square and coloured an unpleasant shade of green.

"But isn't that rather self-defeating?" Patrick was saying. "I mean, once the target is hit, as it inevitably has to be, then there is no more leader."

"Oh, but the men respond to that with increased fervour, better fighting. 'Revenge the General!' they cry."

"So, what did Brock's men do, after he died?"

"Well, they ran about shouting, 'Revenge the General!' for a while ... a few attempted to rush up the Heights.

Then they retreated, took Brock's body back to the flower garden. It's at the old Hamilton house – the garden, I mean. I really must take you there some time."

"They took him back to the flower garden?"

"Yes, and then they made one last valiant attempt to capture Queenston Heights."

"And?"

"Complete chaos, severed limbs, death, the usual."

Fleda searched her memory for another verse.

"But don't you see," David continued, "the whole thing was so wonderful. A young country like ours needs dead heroes. Someone to mourn. Someone to make a monument for."

"Yes, but he was English."

"Only while he was alive. After that, he became entirely Canadian. Not that he ever wanted to be, Lord knows ... but that's of little consequence. Canada claimed him and nothing will ever change that. 'Push on, brave York Volunteers!'"

David held his clenched fist in the air for a moment, and then laughed, finding himself in a ridiculous posture.

Fleda sang, her voice becoming gradually louder:

> God send us men with hearts ablaze
> All truth to love, all wrong to hate
> These are the patriots nations need
> These are the bulwarks of the state

David finally looked in her direction. "Fleda, for heaven's sake, what ... ?"

But Patrick interrupted. "I believe I am a pacifist," he said. "I believe that nothing could induce me to place my body in the direct line of fire."

"It depends," said David, "on what you are fighting for." Actually, he didn't care at all what they were fighting for as long as he could write about it afterwards, but he knew it was important to have something to be fighting for.

"What *were* they fighting for?" Patrick wondered out loud. "Were they fighting against the Americans, for Canada, against Napoleon, for the Empire ... I could never figure it out. I mean, either way we lose, right? We're either the property of one nation or another. We're either Americans or we're British, the only difference being that, after these conflicts, some of us are dead."

"I believe that they were fighting for their own country, the Canadian militia, the Indians," David's voice was beginning to rise. "They may not have known this at the beginning of the conflict, but by the time it was over they knew. They knew they had a country. It was all vague before that, but after ... after, they became a race!"

Fleda began to march around, slowly circling the men. She remembered having felt like this when she was a child, annoyed by adults in rooms and their serious conversations, their orderly behaviour. It occurred to her that her activities were childish, but nothing in her wanted to stop. David was noticing, was beginning to become distracted, but Patrick was lost, out there somewhere, imagining battlefields.

"Battlefields are beautiful," said Patrick, "when the grass comes back. You can see the marks of fighting but they are so benign ... like scars ... no ... smoother than scars. More like memories. Battlefields are so soft, after the grass comes back."

He was really speaking to himself, but David responded. "They should be preserved. We never preserve anything. I want to make a museum ... a better museum. Can't get anyone to preserve anything. There is Brock's monument, of course, but even it has been blown up once."

"There are these wounds in the earth and then the grass comes and covers it all up, like skin, without scars."

"On the other hand, you could hardly blame the Fenians," said David, not listening at all to Patrick. "The Irish certainly have suffered, have been the victims of an overbearing aggressive imperialistic neighbour. The Irish and the Canadians have much in common and will have a great deal more unless we are very careful."

Lord, thought Fleda, these theories ... no humans there at all. No actual people in these landscapes. What about the pain?

"There is that tower at Lundy's Lane," David continued. "But what, tell me, do you see from it? Butcher shops, funeral establishments, greengrocers. And the part of the battlefield that *is* visible isn't even properly marked. It's scandalous!"

The child in Fleda, meanwhile, had decided to take a slightly different tack. She wanted a response from Patrick and now knew she would have to address him directly in order to receive it. Moving closer to that place where he sat, she sang softly, confidentially, wickedly:

> *Though your sins be scarlet*
> *They shall be as snow, as snow*
> *Though they be red, like crimson*
> *They shall be as wool.*

This was a verse she had whispered to herself as a child before going to sleep, so that she could enjoy, in the dark, the wonderful pictures it brought into her imagination: sheep stained bright red, the sinful, bloody scarlet hearts depicted in Papist lithographs, a pair of bright red mittens lying in a snowdrift, white sheep sinfully butchered, stained this time irregularly with their own blood. All this and more ... images of red-hot coals and of scarlet flowers opening, of mouths moistening and of arteries pumping. As a child, she had loved this verse.

The effect on Patrick was instant, though subtle. She saw him wince and then send a brief, chilling glance in her direction. He turned back to David, hoping, she suspected, that if he shut her out entirely, she would stop. She should stop. At another moment she might have even tried to stop. But it was out of her hands now. These crazy hymns she had memorized as a child were taking over. She sang the verse again louder now, but still directed towards Patrick. He was not looking at David any more. His gaze was fixed instead on his hands, his face and neck beginning to colour.

"*Though your sins be like scarlet,*" she began again. She was unwilling to give it up, the anger she suddenly felt, once again, towards him, towards his own vain masculine will.

Then, inexplicably, in mid-verse, she relaxed, became composed, uncaring. She shrugged and turned away from both men, the neutrality of the word *wool* still hanging in the air and finally entering her mind.

She stopped, at that moment, responding to either one of them.

I

*The child was not in the cupboard when she went to look for him there. Maud stood, with a thundering heart, in the doorway, allowing her eyes to adjust to the darkness.

The first thing she saw was the tall, tidy pile of empty canvas sacks, each one about a foot square, which occupied the corner opposite where she stood. She knew they were empty.

Then she saw that the shelves lining the walls were covered with shoe boxes ... objects that had never before filled this space. All the labels on all the shelves had been removed. She noticed, however, that they, too, were piled neatly on the near end of a middle shelf, very close to where her hands now rested.

The child, she supposed, had rescued the boxes from the back of the store two doors down, and kept them hidden. Kept them hidden until the hour arose when he felt the need of them.

Now that her eyes had focused, she began to inspect the contents of these boxes. One held tie-pins, another held buttons. She knew these items. She had recorded them. Another held rings, another was full of watches. A box at the end, larger than the rest, was filled to capacity with teeth, false and otherwise. The light that moved into the cupboard from the hall glittered on gold fillings. There was another box for brooches and still another for hairpins. Maud had not noticed until then how spider-like they were, lying piled together with their legs entangled.

She now saw that the tickets in the sunroom were merely a clue; a fragment of the great number of tickets which were packed together on a bottom shelf in their own special box. They were of such a variety that they might have been able to tell someone other than Maud a great deal about the personality of their owner. Some were mangled, some were folded, some looked as though they had never been touched, some were soiled from incessant handling. Some looked bleached by exposure to water, others appeared to have miraculously avoided any contact with the water at all.

All hope of redistributing this incredible classification process lost, Maud sat on a low stool in the twilight of the closet and considered the possessions of drowned men; how they always carried similar objects in their pockets. Yet, it was the crack in the cuff-link that would allow some relative to identify a body the earth had already, mercifully, taken care of. But rarely did that relative appear. These wild, violent deaths were too grotesque, Maud imagined, to be faced. How were they explained in distant parlours? There were, of course, recipes for disappearance: he went out to buy a newspaper and never returned, he vanished in a snowstorm, he was stolen by gypsies, captured by the fairies, enchanted by a wood nymph on the eve of his marriage.

Maud picked a shoe-box arbitrarily from a shelf directly in front of her. It was filled with pill boxes – round, square, octagonal, rectangular, silver, gold, tin, monogrammed, painted, rusted. She opened one of them. Two round pink tablets looked up at her like a pair of small enchanted eyes . . . like the eyes of a tiny demon.

She leaned back against the wall and closed her eyes. Thousands of small objects floated across her mind, sometimes in conjunction with the words she had written describing them. Some lovely cameos from the necks of young, drowned, probably pregnant girls . . . a variety of timepieces, shoelaces, earrings. Once she had found a bird's nest in a woman's apron pocket. Where, she wondered was that now? How had the child classified it? Surely there was never more than one. She had found books too. Oddly enough, when they weren't guide books they were mostly poetry or prayers. Small books that fit neatly into the breast pocket of a jacket.

Then there were the items the river itself placed in pockets, the river and the rapids; a variety of stones, sticks, sometimes even small fish. One man carried a dead mouse in his pants' pocket. Maud could never decide whether he had brought it with him to the river or whether the river had given it to him. There were tin cans and the bones of whistling swans, sometimes feathers, very occasionally a flower.

When she opened her eyes, the child was standing in the doorway gazing at her. Lit from behind, his hair looked like a brilliant halo surrounding his head, and from inside the gloom of the cupboard Maud perceived that he was the possessor of all the light and that it was she, not he, that had been the dark wall. She had never, since her husband's death, allowed the child access to the other, brighter side of that masonry, she had never allowed him to try to pull it down. Now the child had caused all the objects that surrounded her, all the relics she had catalogued, to lose their dreadful power. He had shown her what they really were: buttons, brooches, tie-clips, garters . . . merely objects.

"Dreaming," he said to her.

"Dreaming," she agreed, rising slowly from the stool.

His hair, when she laid her hands on it, felt warm, soft, alive.

✵

In those last, strange days of summer, everything lost colour.

The air was heavy, full of moisture, with odd gusts of wind so turgid they were like damp blankets flattening the grass. Yet, no rain and no spray from the whirlpool, as though it hadn't the strength to send its white messages up the cliff.

At night, the wind shouldered its way through the pine trees and moved solidly against the tent until it bowed under the pressure. Sometimes it slid through the flaps at the front and, for a moment or two, the interior was like the sail of a ship curving out towards the dark. On these occasions, the oil lamps would be extinguished, leaving Fleda fighting through black and then fumbling with damp, unwilling matches. This wind had no song, she decided, hardly any sound. It was more like what the medievalists called a humour. Something fighting for your body or your soul. It was a noiseless texture, like the breath of a great invisible beast panting, always at the back of your neck so that when you turned to face it, it turned too.

During the day, the wind brought, rather than blew away, the thick mists which were responsible for turning everything grey. And even this was like an attitude or an act of will. When Fleda concentrated, she knew there was colour. She could look at the poplar trees and know they had been green, know they were turning yellow. But the wind, the weather, moaned grey with such consistency it was eventually all she could see.

She was sometimes alone at night now; David working in the rooms in town finishing his tract for the Historical Society. Patrick visiting less and less and gone permanently even when he was there.

The last time, he had come down through the wind and had sat silent in the tent, now picking up a book, now running his hands nervously through his hair, his confident chatter of the previous week completely eliminated. Soon the surrounding air, already heavy with the weather, became hard and still between them ... the only movement caught in canvas, responding to the dogged advances of the wind outside.

He would not speak to her, would not look at her. Alone with her he made it clear it was *she* he desired to be absent from. He was like the weight of the wind, rubbing against the tent, entering for a few disastrous moments, putting out all the lights, gone by the time they are lit again. Gone, but still a constant presence. The interrupted gesture, the words not spoken. She began to associate him with the great weight of this inconclusive wind. There seemed to be no end to it. And there seemed to be no reason.

She remembered the afternoon in July when she had cut her hair; how he had walked away with his hands and his pockets full of it, leaving some behind on branches as he passed by, and how it had glowed there, almost red in the rays of the sun, almost red like his own. She had been delighted by the idea, the image, the colour. But now, if the event were to happen again, the hair would hang neutral and grey on grey branches.

She had tried, recently, several measures to shut the man she remembered out. As if the trappings of her sex were to blame, she began to wear David's trousers and old flannel shirts. She cut her hair again, this time to above her shoulders.

This facilitated her work around the acre, clearing and the planting of bulbs, and made it much easier to climb back up the bank when she had finished fishing in the whirlpool. But undressing at night, when she caught glimpses of her breasts and thighs in the glass, she understood that this desire of hers had not diminished, had only become less centralized ... an idea that had become part of the grey landscape in which she lived. This landscape now soundless, heavy with anxiety and seemingly endless.

Yet, an idea was forming, taking vague shape. Departure. She could no longer live the closeted life of the recent past.

And she could not live, forever, in the dream house of this grey, obsessive landscape.

1 September 1889

I can't imagine this house any more. David is very pleased with the progress on the coach house ... but I just can't imagine it.

Yesterday, I found the Old River Man's cave, halfway around the whirlpool. It was filled with gigantic fishing equipment. Soon it will be time for the bass. This cave seemed better. I wanted to stay there. People did once, but not on this continent.

Last week Patrick was talking about cave paintings made by savages years and years ago ... how fire in the caves makes the painted animals appear to run. He was talking to David. Somewhere in France they have these caves.

Sometimes I listen to them when they talk. Sometimes I don't.

I just can't imagine the house any more, the views from its windows.

Remember the auction sale at the old house?

The only thing I kept was my sterling silver tea service and place settings. Everything else was scattered out on the

lawn around the house, destined for the kitchens and par-
lours of strangers.

David promised that in the new house all the furniture
would be modern.

As if I wanted furniture now, or anything else. The
silver stays in darkness, locked in a vault in town.

I don't want it either. I've forgotten which fork is used
for what. I couldn't survive an afternoon tea. It took no
time for all of that to fade away.

Remember manners?

When do you say "please?" When do you say "thank
you?" When, exactly, did I stop wanting to say either?

The men keep wanting to build things; to order lumber,
hire workmen, draft plans, take measurements. They keep
wanting to deliver concrete messages and plan battles.

I think about Laura Secord living for sixty more years in
the same house, dreaming of one long walk she took in the
wilderness, telling the story, over and over to herself, to
anyone else who would listen.

Nobody understood. It wasn't the message that was
important. It was the walk. The journey.

Setting forth.

ℐ

*P*atrick's whole life had been a departure from certain dramas which should have been his destiny. A dance in which the partners turn away.

In the Gatineaus it had been weather; snow stinging his face, his eyes, the relentless cold. Yet, he wanted to approach the forests in winter, wanted to document, somehow, their strength. But after half an hour he would weaken, return to his wife, to the fire.

Every fibre in his body longed for and feared magnificent dramas. He would sometimes shake his head in disbelief concerning the strength of his fear and the weakness of his persistent longing.

Now he was standing right at the edge of the magnificent theatre that was the whirlpool, trying to steady himself to enter the current. He knew the water at the edge was tremendously gentle. Reflected leaves and subtle green ripples. If you ignored the distance to the other side, the water right in front of you was harmless and predictable. Hardly even a rumour of the whirlpool.

So many decisions concerning this river . . . how to enter . . . where to cross . . . whether to turn away from it entirely. Still, it was decipherable once you had the knowledge. Here there was the whirlpool, a few miles further, swift current, further up, rapids, and even further, the giant cataract – a natural disaster, or wonder, depending how you looked at it.

It was early morning. Fleda would be waking now inside the tent, her limbs unfolding from sleep like a flower. In Ottawa, his wife would be unfolding too. All over this time zone women would be awakening, opening up to the day. They filled his brain now. There was something in him that wanted to embrace them all, and then there was something else, stronger, which turned towards denial.

He stepped towards the river. The sound it made was like a woman's breath near his shoulder, incredibly gentle and quiet and calling. And then this fear of any action concerning the river, as if it were a woman. He who had been such a swimmer. The approach was so smooth, so lacking in hazards you could scarcely tell where the earth ended and the water began.

Looking across the distance of the river to the foreign country on the other side, Patrick considered how there was always a point where one set of circumstances ended and another began. Boundaries, borderlines, territories. This swim would be a journey into another country, a journey he would choose to make in full knowledge that he had no maps, that he hardly spoke the language. Then he realized that the river belonged to no country and that fact made the whole space alien to him.

Still, he wanted to swim.

He walked away from the river through a narrow, dark ravine which became wider as it approached the incline. Here, oddly shaped rocks, left from the ice age, filled the gully and covered the slopes of the bank in random fashion, having been frozen in place in the midst of a tremendous natural upheaval. Hanging down towards these, sometimes covering them, were twisted vines, some as thick as his wrist. The ground at his feet was dark, damp, and filled in spots with tiny streams, all heading for the river, the whirlpool.

He began to notice the roots of the trees that grew there. They gripped the edge of the bank, grew right over the boulders and dug their roots eagerly into the ground wherever they could find it. He could see in them the shapes of serpents and remembered the woman with her black umbrella, thrusting it through the foliage near the ground, looking nervously for rattlers. She doesn't look for them any more, he thought. Whatever that fear was then, it's gone now.

It was not like his fear, not permanent.

He remembered all the times he had returned from the river, remembered that the climb back up the bank was difficult, left your heart pounding in your ears, roaring in your ears like the noise of the whirlpool, the rapids. Patrick sat down on one of the black irregular rocks. He sat there, just listening to the water that he could not see.

Here, in this dark gully, the noise could be any sound at all, could be a collection of streetcars, a symphony of bassoons, the wings of a thousand dark birds migrating. It could be a giant arm of ice moving over the landscape, or any number of suspension bridges falling into the gorge. Or it could be crowds, the incessant murmur of hundreds of people. Or the reverse, a negative sound, the sound of the silence when the crowds have disappeared; a vacuum of sound . . . neutral, harmless.

Patrick listened, choosing the vacuum, letting the peace of it hang in his mind. Behind him the bank, the path leading to the top, the woman a hundred yards to the right of that. Beyond her, a path that led to the road and eventually to the strange child. Patrick chose the vacuum, the neutrality. The softness of water and the sound it makes, the places it goes. All decisions having been made thousands of years ago.

The fear cleared. His spine relaxed. His hands hung limply

over his knees. He sat peacefully on the old black rock for a long time.

Then he rose to his feet and walked, through the dark ravine, back to the river.

∬

The Old River Man was lying on his stomach on a huge flat rock which jutted out over the water. Around him stunning scenery – cliffs striped by the ice age and an expanse of water moving from the rapids to the whirlpool. To his left, carefully wedged between two smaller rocks, was the bottle, three-quarters empty now, the label ragged where his thumbnail had torn it, over and over, as he drank. Lying on Rattler Rock (Reptile Rock) in the sun.

It was rumoured that hundreds of years before, lizards and snakes had sunned themselves there in late summer, passing into the kind of lethargy only a reptile can muster. Only a reptile or a river man with a full bottle, emptying.

He was halfway through the quart when he spotted it out there, floating around and around. Instantly, the alcoholic fog left his brain, his eyes focused. He pulled himself to his feet with a groan.

The place where he kept his equipment was, fortunately, not far. He slipped between the two large rocks forming the enclosure. Even in the gloom, he was able to find exactly what he was looking for. He emerged a few moments later with several sturdy long poles, some wire, and rope, and a large hook.

Now he was back on the rock, on his stomach, with all the equipment wired together into a sort of enormous fishing pole with a good length of rope, followed by the hook, at the end.

"Goddamn my father's black cat's ass!" He missed the target for the fifth time. After the third time he had taken yet another generous swig from the bottle, licking the hand afterwards that he had used to wipe the spillage from his chin. This time he merely cursed and adjusted his position on the rock's surface, waiting like a hunter for the next revolution of the whirlpool.

It mattered little to him whether the object he was after was animal or mineral, dead or alive. He had, in his day, performed many successful rescue missions, would have been a local hero if he could have played that role. But he wasn't concerned with that. He was concerned with whiskey and the river. Essentially he felt it was the river he was rescuing by removing foreign objects from it.

The trees along the banks on the other side could fool you. They were at that stage when their colour was the same as in springtime. You might think they were beginning, instead of beginning to end. But the River Man knew that this was almost autumn ... followed by winter and ice in the river. The water didn't fool him either and it never had. That's what made him different.

He flung the pole out into the whirlpool one more time. It was as if everything around him was drunk except for this small area of concentration. Everything was a blur except for this bundle of flesh and clothing caught in the current.

He felt a tug on his pole. The hook had made contact. "Easy does it, Charlie," he whispered as he began to pull his equipment into shore.

His attention was now occupied by descending from Rattler Rock without letting his catch escape. One awkward move and the whole tedious process would begin over again. Once he had lost not only the body, but his equipment as well. At that point he had been angry enough to tear the whole goddamned escarpment down. But you never really lost anything in the whirlpool forever. Eventually it came back around again. All it took was time, patience, and a new hook.

The body was coming in nicely.... The hook had connected, amazingly enough, with belt buckle. The River Man shook his head. He had never seen this happen before. This way the body was being drawn forward from its centre, the rope looking like a thick umbilical cord, the limbs trailing loosely, slightly behind the torso.

On the opposite shore the River Man could see the red hat of a man who was fishing for a more conventional catch.

This one hadn't been in the river long, he could see that. He hoisted the body up onto the stone beach and returned to the cave to fetch the old tarpaulin to cover it up. Three small boys appeared out of nowhere to watch his activities. "Keep an eye on it," he said.

The River Man wrapped his fist firmly around his bottle and headed along the shore towards the path that would take him up the bank into the world.

∅

On a stump outside the tent, Major David McDougal sat waiting for his wife. He was beginning to become concerned. Already half an hour past the dinner hour and no wife, never mind no food. Punctuality was a word that Major David McDougal had understood completely, it would seem, since the day he was born. Where was his wife?

She had wandered off before, of course, but never for this long. Often, she went to some distant part of the woods to write in that damned book of hers or to gather who knows what number or variety of flowers, and for who knows what reasons. But she understood his need for punctuality and always returned in time. Why should she choose this day to make an exception to rules she had learned so well?

Nothing, McDougal concluded, was predictable about women, including their predictability.

He rose and stomped testily into the tent, to look inside; something that had not occurred to him he should do until now. He would find that notebook of hers and read it. What *had* she been scribbling, anyway, all those afternoons at the edge of the bank? He looked all over the tent, even under the bed and in the laundry hamper, which he noticed had not yet received yesterday's socks and underwear, and found no notebook. So, she was off somewhere writing, he decided. And her Browning books were gone as well. She was off somewhere writing, reading Browning, and recording her elevated thoughts. Women had such vague and dreary ways of wasting time. He would give her the Laura Secord lecture when she returned. What if *she* had decided to mope dreamily around reading poetry instead of delivering messages. What would have happened *then*.

He imagined his wife's contrite expression as he, kindly but firmly, pointed this out to her.

Back outside, he moved around to the opposite side of the tent to gaze at the frame of the carriage house. The sun threw a gridwork of straight timber shadows all over the foliage around him. Architecture making its geometric statement on the landscape. The solidity of the work pleased the major. He knew the beams weren't going anywhere, that they would be there for a long, long time.

After nightfall his unease changed gears, shifted dramatically into panic. Something had happened, he was sure of it. He had already broken open his emergency supply of whiskey and his thoughts were becoming somewhat disjointed. He was having horrifying fantasies concerning treacherous acts involving male American tourists, whom, he believed, even while he was sober, you should never trust. Any American was bred to want to take over things; your water supply, your mineral deposits, your entire country, your wife. "The bastards," he mumbled quietly to himself, ominously eyeing the 1812 musket he kept in a corner of the tent for just such occasions. And, even worse, the thought struck him suddenly, she might have been kidnapped by an American military historian who had heard about his work and was even now trying to obtain, by God knows what form of terrifying means, information concerning his views on the Siege of Fort Erie.

Either you tell me how many pages he has written, Madam, or I will rip open that muddy calico dress of yours from the neck to the knees.

"The swine," growled McDougal, promising himself to look into the matter of armed sentries at all border crossings.

By ten o'clock, he had finished his emergency supply of whiskey and was working on his emergency supply of gin. He was ready to declare war. Something American had happened to his wife ... there was no other possible explanation.

A third of the way through the gin, he began to become embarrassed. How does one look for a lost wife? How does one admit to the authorities that she was left alone in the woods, a perfect lure for the ever-present enemy? How does one convince the authorities that something American has happened to your wife and that action would have to be taken immediately? It was hopeless. They would let the Yanks take anything, everything, and never bat an eyelash.

Large, angry tears filled his eyes. The tent became blurry. It was as though McDougal's world were evaporating right before his eyes, cartwheeling vaguely away into another nationality, taking everything familiar with it.

The next morning he awoke abruptly from a dream concerning Robert Browning's views of military life and realized his wife was gone. Because he had not undressed the night before, he was able to spring immediately from his bed, leave the tent and rush distractedly into the woods calling her name. Not expecting an answer by now, but calling nonetheless, as people do who have irrevocably lost something. He could actually feel her absence in the atmosphere, feel that the acre was making a statement about the improbability of her ever returning to the spot. It seemed to him absurd that when she was so undeniably gone the kettle and the dish pan should still be where she left them, that the hammock he had placed at the edge of the bank still remained.

Looking from this edge down towards the water, he could see the River Man, a tiny elf, fishing for something with his strange equipment. Then he could see him reeling in his catch. Major McDougal turned away, disallowing the conclusion that was trying to gain entry into his mind. He decided instead to make a thorough search of the woods up and down the bank. Some time later he saw the men descend the bank with their wicker basket. Still he refused to look carefully at the information that was being given to him.

He searched behind every shrub and behind every thicket. He called and called with his best military voice, until his voice left him altogether. It was late in the afternoon before he decided that he would have to visit the funeral home.

As McDougal sat on the streetcar that would take him to Main Street and the undertaker's, a sudden series of memories flashed through his mind concerning an old aunt of his, one he had known only superficially. He recalled, now, how she had died, slowly and in stages, not so much from disease as from withdrawal . . . the whole process taking years.

First, she had refused to visit Toronto ever again, giving up forever her spring and fall shopping trips. But, when several months later, she had decided not to venture beyond her own garden gate, relatives were called upon to do errands for her. David had been one of them. When winter came, she settled into her parlour and her daily path was reduced to that between kitchen and parlour and bedroom.

One day, when he arrived with a loaf of bread, he found her ensconced in her bedroom at two in the afternoon. Claiming that she felt just fine, she announced that the only way she would leave the room would be feet first. At this point she should have died, but she didn't. This stage lasted five years, during which her sole occupation was the ordering of an endless series of bedjackets from Eaton's and Simpsons catalogues. After her death, sixty-seven of these garments were discovered in her bedroom closet and dresser drawers.

Now it occurred to McDougal that his life had been moving down a path which would eventually carry him through the door of his still unconstructed house. And while he had imagined walking through the door of the house, he had never considered stepping back outside. The perimeter of his own life was shrinking. He was just like his barely remembered aunt.

When he arrived at Grady and Son he was startled to find that it was Patrick, rather than his wife, in the basket. The sorrow he had carried with him on the streetcar spilled out now and he began to weep.

"So young," Maud commented sympathetically. "A real tragedy. Was he related to you? Whom should we contact?"

"I don't know where she is," replied McDougal. "I don't know how to contact her at all."

Leaving the undertaking establishment McDougal went directly to the museum to look at ammunition. Bullets, gunflints, grapeshot, cannon-balls, caged and harmless in their glass cabinets.

There was peace here, and the major knew it. Emptied of drama and emotion these artifacts would not be making any further statements, any further journeys. They would remain here now, stunningly innocent and clear, years after their complicated performances involving death and pain. They had become three-dimensional documents locked away in rooms.

McDougal was comforted by the sight of these objects carefully arranged on fabric, safely catalogued and housed. He stayed there with the tips of his fingers resting on the cool glass, looking over his shoulder only once when he thought he might have heard the rustle of a woman's skirt on the oak floor.

✐

The young man was beautiful. Maud had not been prepared for that. The drowning had hardly affected him except to place a thin, hardly noticeable film across his eyes. But that was merely death. The rest of him was undamaged, perfect. He was like a dead child.

She had seen the film before, many times. It reminded her of the caul which had partially covered her child's face at birth, except that here, in death, it only covered the eyes. The caul was supposed to make the baby exceptionally lucky, all through his life. Her mother-in-law had said so . . . had said also that it was a preservative against drowning. Later, it seemed that many of the river bodies carried this charm, fragments of it, in their eyes.

A gift that had come too late.

Her mother-in-law had wanted to keep the caul. She told Maud that in Ireland it would be dried and cut up into pieces so that each member of the family might share in the luck. They would carry fragments of it around in their back pockets, to ward off curses, to ward off drowning. Maud could never understand this. She was revolted by the membrane and insisted that it should be disposed of. Until the moment of her death, Maud's mother-in-law maintained that the baby was odd because his caul had been taken from him and destroyed.

Maud was no longer in mourning. She had dressed today for the first time in bright yellow, the colour of her autumn flowers. She had discarded everything, all the crape, all the mauve and black and white cotton, all the kept things connected with death.

She and the child had carried the boxes of teeth and keys and rings, tie-clips, shoelaces, and laundry-markers out to the wagon. Jesus Christ and God Almighty would take whatever Sam and Jas and Peter didn't want off to the dump.

And then they had brought in the beautiful drowned man.

Gazing at his pale corpse, now, Maud heard her mother-in-law's voice again ... the way she said the word *caul*, the word *blessed*, the word *cursed*. Beside her the child stood transfixed, his face pale and shining. He said the word "man" three times, slowly and deliberately and then the word "swim." With one hand, he reached towards the corpse's cuff but Maud pulled him back, closer to her own warm body.

Fleda had set her little boats adrift and had walked away. She followed Laura Secord's route but she carried with her no deep messages.

At the abandoned river the sun slipped behind a cloud. "Dreamhouse," "Adonais," "Angel," and "Warrior" floating on the surface changed, simultaneously, from white to grey. Shadow covered the whirlpool.

⌀

❦ Epilogue ❧

Robert Browning lay dying in his son's Venetian palazzo. Half of his face was shaded by a large velvet curtain which was gathered by his shoulder, the other half lay exposed to the weak winter light. His sister, son, and daughter-in-law stood at the foot of the bed nervously awaiting words or signs from the old man. They spoke to each other silently by means of glances or gestures, hoping they would not miss any kind of signal from his body, mountain-like under the white bedclothes. But for hours now nothing had happened. Browning's large chest moved up and down in a slow and rhythmic fashion, not unlike an artificially manipulated bellows. He appeared to be unconscious.

But Browning was not unconscious. Rather, he had used the last remnants of his free will to make a final decision. There were to be no last words. How inadequate his words seemed now compared to Shelley's experience, how silly this monotonous bedridden death. He did not intend to further add to the absurdity by pontificating. He now knew that he had said too much. At this very moment in London, a volume of superfluous words was coming off the press. All this chatter filling up the space of Shelley's more important silence. He now knew that when Shelley had spoken it was by choice and not by habit, that the young man's words had been a response and not a fabrication.

235

He opened his eyes a crack and found himself staring at the ceiling. The fresco there moved and changed and finally evolved into Shelley's iconography – an eagle struggling with a serpent. *Suntreader*. The clouds, the white foam of the clouds, like water, the feathers of the great wings becoming lost in this. *Half angel, half bird*. And the blue of the sky, opening now, erasing the ceiling, limitless so that the bird's wing seemed to vaporize. *A moulted feather, an eagle feather*. Such untravelled distance in which light arrived and disappeared leaving behind something that was not darkness. *His radiant form becoming less radiant*. Leaving its own natural absence with the strength and the suck of a vacuum. No alternate atmosphere to fill the place abandoned. *Suntreader*.

And now Browning understood. It was Shelley's absence he had carried with him all these years until it had passed beyond his understanding. *Soft star*. Shelley's emotions so absent from the old poet's life, his work, leaving him unanswered, speaking through the mouths of others, until he had to turn away from Shelley altogether in anger and disgust. The drowned spirit had outdistanced him wherever he sought it. *Lone and sunny idleness of heaven*. The anger, the disgust, the evaporation. *Suntreader, soft star*. The formless form he never possessed and was never possessed by.

Too weak for anger now, Robert Browning closed his eyes and relaxed his fists, allowing Shelley's corpse to enter the place in his imagination where once there had been only absence. It floated through the sea of Browning's mind, its muscles soft under the constant pressure of the ocean. Limp and drifting, the drowned man looked as supple as a mermaid, arms swaying in the current, hair and clothing tossed as if in a slow, slow wind. His body was losing colour, turning from pastel to opaque, the open eyes staring, pale, as if frozen by an image of the moon. Joints unlocked by moisture, limbs swung easy on their threads of tendon, the spine undulating and relaxed. The absolute grace of this death, that life caught there moving in the arms of the sea. Responding, always responding, to the elements.

Now the drowned poet began to move into a kind of Atlantis consisting of Browning's dream architecture; the unobtainable and the unconstructed. In complete silence the young man swam through the rooms of the Palazzo Manzoni, slipping up and down the staircase, gliding down halls, in and out of fireplaces. He appeared briefly in mirrors. He drifted past balconies to the tower Browning had thought of building at Asolo. He wavered for a few minutes near its crenelated peak before moving in a slow spiral down along its edges to its base.

Browning had just enough time to wish for the drama and the luxury of a death by water. Then his fading attention was caught by the rhythmic bump of a moored gondola against the terrace below. The boat was waiting, he knew, to take his body to the cemetery at San Michele when the afternoon had passed. Shelley had said somewhere that a gondola was a butterfly emerging from a coffin-chrysalis.

Suntreader. Still beyond his grasp. The eagle on the ceiling lost in unfocused fog. *A moulted feather, an eagle feather, well I forget the rest*. The drowned man's body separated into parts and moved slowly out of Browning's mind. The old poet contented himself with the thought of one last journey by water. The coffin boat, the chrysalis. Across the Laguna Morta to San Michele. All that cool white marble in exchange for the shifting sands of Lerici.

ॐ

JANE URQUHART

CHANGING HEAVEN

Ann, a Brontë scholar, retreats from an obsessive affair to *Wuthering Heights* country, there befriending a man who becomes in many ways her saviour. Interwoven with this highly charged story of the present is a strange tale from the past – of balloonist Arianna Ether and her possessive lover. When Arianna attempts a parachute jump from her balloon above Haworth, disaster strikes. Falling to the moors below, she encounters the ghost of Emily Brontë and thereby begins an extraordinary conversation about life, love and tragedy which echoes across the centuries.

'A quirky, intense, lyrical and funny novel'
The Independent on Sunday

'An interesting text on the relationship between literature and the emotions of those who study it'
The Guardian

'Throughout this ambitious and imaginative book, the weather is almost a spiritual being . . . The wind laughs and talks as it weaves together three separate love stories, pointing out those similarities which transcend time and place'
Literary Review

'A complex bridging of three time periods and a melding of the supernatural and the commonplace'
Quill & Quire

WILLIAM RIVIÈRE

WATERCOLOUR SKY

Under the open skies of north Norfolk, the Dobell family seems to lead an idyllic life, the countryside and its sporting pursuits closely interwoven with the very fabric of existence. Yet happiness eludes two generations; only the natural world remains a passion which sustains expectations in this haunting tale of loss and deep but ill-fated emotions.

'Entrancing . . . Rivière's outdoor scenes are superb. Neither Turgenev nor Hemingway could teach him much about evoking field and water'
Michael Barber in The Listener

'Robust yet delicate, like a good wine. I enjoyed it very much'
John Bayley

'A luminous first novel; it's a love story free of any sentimental clutter. And it's the best evocation of East Anglia since Graham Swift's *Waterland*'
Company

'The author has a sensitive pen and an ability to portray his characters as real. Again and again we are rewarded by small epiphanies: love's first kiss, an old man scything, a moment watching ghostly owls crossing an open starry sky'
John Wyse Jackson in The Sunday Times

'A first novel of great promise . . . a beautifully written, melancholy tale'
John Nicholson in The Times